Souls Dow

by

Peter Chegwidden

www.publishnation.co.uk

Chapter One

Barry and Marge Hughes were keen walkers and had been looking forward to their holiday in this part of Countryshire. From the town of Prattle where they were staying they had strolled up the foothills to the east, climbed across the rugged, rocky peaks beyond, and were now gazing down at the splendid Flemm valley beyond.

In a day they could do little more than reach the first settlement before returning to their accommodation. They started their short downward descent to pause briefly at High Stayckes and admire the lovely olde-worlde stone buildings prior to heading back to the hills. They photographed one or two of the higgledy-piggleldy buildings, properties seemingly just dumped wherever they might land in a hamlet without shape or good order.

For this was the countryside and how they thought the countryside villages should look.

And then the Hughes were gone.

***

High Stayckes

Alfie Barrett had not taken to modern amenities so, despite his cottage having a bathroom and hot water heated by the range, he preferred to take his bath in the lounge. Also being something of a conventional traditionalist Alfie involved his wife, Ethel, in this practice, she having to fetch the tin bath in from the shed and fill it with water, a lengthy process as you might imagine.

Since she also had to subsequently empty the dirty water once he had finished and remove the bath while he drip-dried in front of the range, it will be appreciated Ethel was kept busy as indeed she was much of every day in one way or another.

A keen gardener, enthusiastic and passionate, she lacked any horticultural knowledge to make a success of it and was known

1

to cut down plants just coming into bloom and had once sprayed the roses with the wrong kind of weedkiller. She was unbothered by the results of her efforts assuming all that happened was merely the manifestation of nature at work.

Ethel named their small cottage in High Stayckes '*Alopecia*' in the mistaken belief that it was the Latin name for the marigolds that sometimes appeared in her garden. She and Alfie had been born in the village and had appeared destined for each other from childhood all those many years ago. They had been blessed with four children and in a great rush, there being less than one year between each birth, but their offspring had sprung off to seek employment and pleasure in the big towns and cities.

Alfie had worked on nearby Elppin Farm until retirement came calling and even now often answered the call for a little seasonal assistance from the farmer, rewarded with a little cash in hand, no questions asked.

Now Thursday was his bath night. It always had been.

It wasn't unusual for unsuspecting visitors, such as neighbours, to be escorted by Ethel into the sitting room where they were presented with the sight of her husband immersed in the tub, or for him to join in the conversation from such a position if he was invited to do so. Callers tended to take this all in their stride, especially Mrs Rifle who was prone to pop in Thursdays on the pretext of needing a natter with his wife.

On one occasion she arrived late, coincidently just before he concluded his wash, and while Ethel went and found a towel she was treated to the sight of Alfie standing up stark naked and facing her. Doing all in her power to do anything other than avert her gaze Mrs Rifle took in the treat before her and was disappointed when Ethel returned and covered her husband's modesty and other interesting features.

Not that the event worried or embarrassed either woman; Alfie was Alfie and the village accepted it.

For widowed Ada Rifle the matter had novelty value as she had not only never seen her own husband undressed she had never seen any naked man in the flesh, so to speak, and the experience was uplifting in a way she couldn't readily explain. Of course she'd seen pictures and she'd seen statues, there being plenty of the latter at Bowgher Hall, the early Georgian stately home she'd visited near the town of Bendham.

That night, as she turned out the light and settled down under the blankets, she found herself warmed by the memory of all she had witnessed and passed into the arms of Morpheus with a smile upon her face.

Thus was the scene set for a rather different Sunday afternoon the coming weekend.

Before her Sunday dinner Ada went into action having planned her move with military precision. With great dexterity she took a screwdriver to the hinges on the bedroom door in her own cottage and worked on them until the door stuck fast less than six inches open, then stood back sporting a smile of satisfaction and admiration, task complete.

The Rifles had been a childless couple, but not for the want of trying. What had always upset Ada was that trying was conducted at night and in the dark and she had felt she was missing something, but would never have queried it with Hubert as it wasn't the done thing.

For now the trap was laid, Ada not actually giving any thought to what she would do once she had Alfie Barrett in her lair. All she knew was that she wanted that vision of beauty in her boudoir, the bedroom being where she believed assignations of a naughty and personal nature normally took place.

Mid-afternoon found her knocking on the door of Alopecia and asking Ethel if she could borrow Alfie as her bedroom door had become stuck and she had not the strength to do anything about it.

Playing the helpless little old lady worked a dream for Alfie was with her in an instant, only too pleased to try and help, and gathering up a couple of basic tools he was soon on the way to the widow's abode, chatting with her as he went and trying to keep her forlorn spirits up.

She really was playing the part.

Having examined the door he turned to the now excited Ada Rifle.

"Yer 'inges 'ave come loose, m'duck. Don't you worry none. Soon have it fixed." And within a few minutes it was fixed and he stepped into the bedroom, swinging the door a few times to

3

demonstrate job done, at which point, unable to control herself any longer, Ada threw herself at him clasping him around the waist and hugging him tightly. Alfie, with every degree of innocence, assumed this was a worried neighbour showing her relief that her problem had been solved. But Ada had another problem to solve right now.

For she lacked the experience and knowledge of what to do next having never tried to seduce anyone and not even knowing what the word meant. There was only one thing for it. Route one. She released her captive, looked him right in the eyes and spoke with more confidence than she felt, and with a tremble and a plea in her voice.

"Alfie, Alfie, since I saw you getting out of the bath I've longed to see you like that again."

"Only too happy to oblige Ada. Go and run a bath and I'll jump in and get out again."

"No, no, no Alfie. I'm sorry. I meant I want to see you naked. I know I'm not your wife and I'm not entitled to see you undressed but … but … but … but …"

"Oh I see Ada, I see. Well I can't see any 'arm in it, as long as its fer artistic purposes only and there won't be any touchin'….."

"Yes, but there will be. I want to touch you Alfie. I want you to touch me."

"Where do you want to touch me Ada?"

"Here in the bedroom Alfie…."

"Yes I know that, but what part of me? And what part of you wants touching?"

She stepped back, a look of vexation appearing on her face. What *did* she actually want to touch? She wasn't sure, and furthermore she had no idea what a woman did once she was touching any particular part of a man. What did she want Alfie to touch? Good heavens, even Hubert had never touched anything he shouldn't.

And in that moment she realised her plan was undone. This whole business was a world of mystery, a world she had never been part of, and in her misery she burst into tears. Alfie, a kind and compassionate man, immediately put his arms around her and squeezed her gently as the tears fell and she tried to speak through the sobs.

"Oh Alfie, Alfie, I've no idea what I'm doing. I don't even know what I do want. I'm so naïve in these matters. Oh please help me, please, please help me." And the tears became a flood as her would-be paramour comforted her in his arms, and in such a position came to grasp what Mrs Rifle was up to. Always willing to help out a friend and neighbour he leaned back slightly and made a suggestion which he hoped might assist the now distraught widow.

"If I'm a-reading you right Ada, you're not sure what 'appens next, so would it help if I seduced *you* now we've got this far?" Slowly the supply of tears lessened and her expression changed to one of puzzlement and bewilderment.

"What does seduced mean Alfie?"

In fairness to the man he was none too clear himself, at least as far as the dictionary definition was concerned, so he pursed his lips as he allowed his thoughts to run amok with all he knew about the art of seduction, when in truth there was precious little subject matter to play with. He made up his mind.

"Well, it's like this Ada. We both get undressed then we kisses each other and then see if there's anything else we want to do, if you understand me." Ada didn't but made no comment. It had never occurred to her that she might need to remove her own clothes and the thought of doing so in front of a neighbour filled her with revulsion. What else could they possibly want to do, she asked herself?

"Oh well Alfie, I don't think so, I really don't think so. I hope you won't be offended?"

"No m'dear, no 'arm done, and you can always pop round next Thursday and see me get out the bath. Eth won't mind." But somehow Ada knew she wouldn't call in on a Thursday again. Best let sleeping dogs lie, she reasoned.

Declining a proffered cup of tea, suggested as a means of compensation in Ada's eyes, Alfie collected his tools, used and unused, and departed as cheerily as he'd arrived.

"No 'arm done," he'd added as his parting words as he waved goodbye to an utterly confused Mrs Rifle who stood on her doorstep feeling anything but disappointed, and wondering what

5

on earth all the fuss might've been about. Yes, she resolved, leave well alone. No harm done.

Alfie Barrett whistled a happy tune as he made his way home. Dodged a bullet there me old son, he congratulated himself, which is just as well, he agreed with himself, since I can't say I'd have known what to do next. Bit of a do that, bit of a do. Anyway, safe at last. Kept me powder dry. Might try seducing Ethel tonight. Yes that's it. Seduce the missus. That's what missuses are for!

And he chuckled as he reached the gate knowing full well Mrs Barrett would go unseduced and they would both be the better for it.

Tomorrow he was going to take the local bus to the next village, Nether Noing, to see his old mate Charlie Punge. He'd tell Charlie all about it and they could have a good laugh.

Chapter Two

The local bus service, connecting all the villages with each other and with the market town of Great Barsterd, ran to a timetable described by users as a complete work of fiction.

It was operated by a man from High Stayckes rejoicing in the name of Oliver Buckett, and only ran at all if he could find the starting handle, this implement having a number of alternative uses in the Buckett household and often being in the possession of Mrs B for such purposes.

The small minibus looked like a relic from a bygone era, such as the stone age, and it was widely rumoured to run on elastic rather than diesel. But Oliver was proud of it. Perhaps through innocent naivety or simply unconscious self-deprecating humour, the vehicle was emblazoned with the owner's names in large, bold letters along both sides.

'O. Buckett' it read, which led to villagers adopting the term into their local dialect as a synonym for "Oh dear" or similar.

Today it was twenty five minutes late leaving High Stayckes which its only passenger, Alfie Barrett, regarded as something of an achievement and a positive step towards future reliability.

"Olly, I can't find my blinking bus pass," he said as he boarded.

"That's alright Alfie, I can't find my blinking ticket machine!" the driver responded.

Then with a chug and a splutter the minibus wandered off at a sedate pace in the direction of Nether Noing.

***

Nether Noing

Charlie Punge apologised for keeping Alfie waiting on the doorstep.

"Sorry Alf. Just had to give me daughter a spanking."

The daughter was grinning from ear to ear, suggesting her father was only joking, yet Alfie couldn't help thinking she

7

looked very rosy cheeked, no doubt in all respects. He might also have considered it a light-hearted remark bearing in mind Eileen Punge was forty-seven and therefore largely beyond parental guidance, except by mutual consent of course.

Eileen was unwed. As a teenager she had fallen helplessly in love with Jed and sworn to adore and worship him to her dying day just as she had sworn to make him happy beyond words, and to cater for his every need. Folk felt they made an ideal, dedicated and beautiful couple but as Jed was the farmer's horse marriage was unlikely and probably illegal anyway.

Charlie had been widowed when Eileen was just seven and appeared to have done a splendid job raising his daughter single-handed, juggling fatherhood with his work as a shepherd. There had been frequent sightings of him and Eileen up on the hillside tending the flock, and as she blossomed into an attractive if buxom young lady she never once hankered to be away from her rustic idyll or from the sheep.

Perhaps unsurprisingly she eschewed the idea of a career away from Flemmdale and chose to qualify as plumber, her business being named 'Punge Plumbing', and she had been remarkably successful in her pursuit possessing skills that became all but legendary. Often coarsely referred to as the 'Wench with a wrench' she tackled all tasks with strength and gusto and exceptionally good cheer. No plumbing job defeated her.

Although Jed was long gone there was no question of her remaining faithful to his memory and she had set about finding a substitute lover and potential husband the same way she approached her work. With strength, gusto and exceptionally good cheer.

The fact she had not yet accomplished her aim was dismissed crudely by locals who believed she had not found a man who was, to use a vulgar colloquialism, hung like a horse, whereas the truth of the matter was that she enjoyed playing the field and was blowed if she was going to stop now while there were still single men in the valley she had not sampled.

This morning to she was off down the lane to fix a gentleman's ballcock.

Walter Pratt had moved to Nether Noing upon retirement, leaving the busy town of Bendham behind and escaping to the country, coincidently escaping the painful memories of the home he'd shared for so many years with his beloved late wife Hilda, a home where they'd raised their three children and seen them set off far and wide to start families of their own.

"Morning Wally," Eileen called out as he opened the front door.

"Hello Eileen. Thank you for coming. Come on in, come on in." She followed him into the narrow hall as he continued his dialogue.

"I had a leak in the toilet last night," he explained, "and I think it's the cistern overflowing. Come upstairs and I'll show you.

She checked the offending cistern and swiftly reached a decision.

"You haven't got a ballcock Wally. Not as such. It's a kind of valve system, much the same really, but a bit more sophisticated until it doesn't work anyway and then it's just as stupid as the old-fashioned equipment. No problem. I'll change it for you. Only take a mo. Now where's your stopcock?"

"Oh. No idea. What's a stopcock and how would I recognise it?"

Eileen sucked air in through clenched teeth. Oh blow, she thought, this could end up taking some time, and with that explained, as politely as she could, the role of the stopcock and why it was vital to know where it was located.

"Ah," he responded, "I might be able to help you there. I have a small hole with a lid on it between the cottage and the garage. Never looked. Never thought it necessary. Might that be where the cock it is?" Eileen nodded.

Wally's small hole did indeed turn out to be where the stopcock was although Eileen took a while to free it. With that she was no time changing the valve and then turning the water back on to test it. Perfect! Meanwhile Wally had been making coffee which they now sat in the kitchen to enjoy.

In his naturally harmless, innocent and otherwise charming way he asked a question.

"Eileen, do you have a small hole with a cock in it?" Spluttering into her coffee mug she pondered how she might best

9

answer this and finally ignoring all the possibilities that had travelled unchecked through her mind gave the simplest of answers.

"Yes Wally." There seemed nothing to add, at least not out loud, believing the answers to what was basically a two-part question were 'no' and 'not often enough' respectively.

He settled her bill, inclusive of a generous tip which she tried in vain to refuse, and set sail for her next call. Wally Pratt, she thought to herself, what a good name for such an innocent and lovely old man!

It was but a short stroll to 'The Grapes' – a splendid detached house in extensive grounds. Looking at the nameplate on the gate she observed that some wag, probably a ne'er-do-well village child, had scratched away part of the letter 'a' so that it read 'The Gropes'. Eileen sniggered. As this was the home of the dale's doctor the word grope could be easily misapplied to his profession she reasoned in a sniggering kind of way.

Dr Rummage was out on call so she was greeted at the front door by the doctor's wife, a large, red-faced and well-rounded lady wearing a shockingly short skirt for one of such size and age. Full of good humour and bonhomie, bursting with happiness, laughter always ready to eagerly escape her chubby lips, Bernice Rummage was nonetheless a no-nonsense woman of strong character and a leading light in the theatre of feminism who would suffer no fool gladly. Outspoken, she was not the sort of person to try and do battle with.

Although Eileen was not a central heating engineer the purpose of her visit was to bleed the radiators, this task being beyond the doctor and his wife. It had amused Eileen to think of a physician needing bleeding, a practice long ago abandoned by the medical profession.

Bernice escorted her around the house as the plumber bled each radiator in turn. She would irritate her visitor from time to time by calling her a plumbette rather than plumber. The irritation came not from the term, which Eileen felt pleasantly endearing, but the knowledge that Bernice was a forthright feminist.

Dr Rummage stood in complete contrast to his wife. Stick thin, tall and slightly bent at the neck he reminded Eileen of the shepherd's crook she had been given by her father and which was a treasured possession, oft employed in days gone by up on the hills minding the sheep. Rummage wore a permanently doleful expression, no doubt engendered by years of subservience to his wife and her cause, an expression suited to imparting bad medical news, but not the good.

Many a patient had recoiled at that expression, fearing the worst, only to be told they were in excellent health or that whatever they suffered from would clear up soon. Here was a man who could lance a boil with consummate ease and a wife who could achieve the same result with just a glance, and neither could bleed their radiators. Still why worry, just call in the plumbette, Eileen concluded.

In the main bedroom the bed was unmade and the sheets, pillows and duvet looked so crumpled Eileen managed to mischievously conjure up a picture of Dr and Mrs Rummage engaged in marital pursuits in a violent and over-excitable manner, believing that Bernice would probably control the entire session whereas it was not beyond reason that this was where the doctor held sway. Maybe he tied his wife up and gagged her, and perhaps she loved it! Wicked thoughts indeed.

Right now as she attended to the radiator Eileen was aware of Bernice breathing very heavily right behind her. As the air escaped with a hiss Eileen wondered what glorious scenes this radiator must've witnessed, as a vision of Mrs Rummage tied and gagged floated through her mind provoking an hilarious picture of her husband taking her pulse, sounding her chest and then giving her something for her headache! And how!

What destroyed the image and also enhanced it in a most unpleasant way was Bernice's next comment.

"Must make the bed when you've gone. What a mess. Trouble is my husband had to give me an enema this morning and I have to confess I'm a bad patient. Y'know, I wriggle a lot, that sort of thing. Sorry, expect that's too much information." And she guffawed in a way that shook the windows and then compounded her offence by continuing in the same vein.

"My husband thinks an enema is a cure for many ails. He's making a house call on a young woman in Little Pryck first thing

11

tomorrow and I bet he gives her one." An enema or what, Eileen queried silently, musing on a range of possibilities.

Paid, the plumbette couldn't wait to be away, afeared for the poor woman in Little Pryck and only too pleased Dr Rummage had never recommended such a course of treatment for any complaint she'd taken to him.

"Hello there Eileen," a disembodied voice called from behind her somewhere. She turned to see Matthew Paynter emerging from behind a building and waving at her. She returned the greeting and the wave and allowed him to catch up with her.

Forever known as Matt Paint he was one single man Eileen had never really got to know, possibly because he worked in Bendham and did not spend much time in Nether Noing. Seizing her opportunity, noting his keenness to converse with her, she elected to go for the jugular, to use an expression, and bluntly asked him for a date. Taken aback at first he soon regained his senses.

"Well Eileen, I think that's a good idea, but do you think we'd be compatible?"

"That's the concept of going on a date, isn't it? Find out about how you get along and at least have a good time in the process."

"Be nice if we thought we'd get along okay anyway. Might save time in the long run, know what I mean?"

"I've got an idea Matt. See them thick bushes over by that tree?" He nodded. She continued.

"Let's pop over there for a few minutes and we can test our compatibility now."

A few minutes later they emerged from the undergrowth both convinced about their compatibility and sizzling with anticipation as they finalised arrangements for their date the following evening, and Eileen found she had a spring in her step she had not enjoyed for some weeks as she made her way to the next call.

By comparison Dr Rummage made his way through a fairly routine, almost boring day and went home for a boring evening and was certainly not sizzling with anticipation although it was true Bernice did have a lovely roast dinner ready him which he enjoyed.

12

He checked his diary. First call tomorrow, Miss Hardshaw, the barmaid in Little Pryck, and sighed at the boring monotony of it all.

Chapter Three

After a peaceful and undisturbed night Dr Rummage rose, washed, shaved and dressed and enjoyed a delicious full-English, secretly pleased his wife's interest in klismaphilia had not surfaced that morning to require a degree of satisfaction that only he could provide.

He climbed into his car and set off the three miles down the lane to the next settlement, Little Pryck, and the home of his first patient, Lucy Hardshaw. The barmaid had become known to regulars at the pub as 'little Luce' on account of her small stature, a nickname she loved.

"I'm a little Luce," she would proudly boast as an encouragement to the plethora of raucous comment that would inevitably follow in both the saloon and public bars.

Pryck referred to the nearby rocky outcrop which the Flemm had to swerve around. Apparently the word pryck was a derivative of an Anglo-Saxon term for any form of large, robust outcrop. Tourists frequently enquired of locals if there was a Great Pryck and a received a variety of answers as you might expect, but there was certainly no village of the name.

***

Little Pryck

The pub where little Luce worked was called the Beau Nidle, named in honour of an 18th century earl of Flemmdale, Richard Nidle, a Georgian dandy whose prime interests were hunting and shooting (especially deer and peasants), and making a nuisance of himself with the ladies.

But he appeared to be successful in his business activities, did not gamble and was a true philanthropist. He employed many more local people than he needed to in his house and estate and paid for a school and medical facilities in Little Pryck. The family moved away in the 19th century and much of the estate was sold off over time.

Eventually Pryck Hall itself was deserted, left to go to ruin, and was then purchased by a well-known television celebrity and completely re-vamped primarily to be used as a venue for the owner's elaborate parties. Fortunately the Hall was sufficient distance away for bashes not to be a trouble to the rural communities. Needless to say the vacuous celebrity kept the name believing it added a certain joie-de-vivre to invitations.

The Beau Nidle was in the hands of Dorothea Dollop and her husband Arthur. She liked to be called by her full name and never answered to Dot, Dotty, Dolly, Thea or any other shortened version.

Some time ago she'd come up with a bright idea.

Being the only pub in the valley it was very popular with tourists especially in the summer and although some of the regulars liked to mingle with the assorted walkers, cyclists and other visitors some did not. Concerned she might lose trade Dorothea adapted a large spare room at the rear of the building into a private bar, fitting an electronic entry system. For a small fee villagers could join for a year and be given a swipe-card to gain automatic admission. The scheme made Mrs Dollop the toast of the dale, and a great deal of profit.

Another reason why the inn was popular with tourists was that it was reputedly haunted.

The building actually dated back to 1547 becoming a tavern in 1784. Around 1625 it was home to two sisters one of whom was jilted at the altar, the other sister eloping with her husband-to-be. The first girl hunted down her sibling and stabbed her to death in front of the man. Having committed this act of sororicide she gave the man the option of handing her over to the authorities or running away with her, so the legend went.

The story suggests she told him he was back where he started. It was her or nothing. After a brief pause for consideration he decided against handing her over thinking that he might just as well make the most of the opportunity presented to him.

They fled to Ireland and history does not relate what happened thereafter. Neither does folklore.

Credence was added to the myth when, around 1814, a writer stayed at the inn and claimed he heard the ghosts of two girls screaming at each other and, when he investigated, saw two figures on the landing struggling and fighting. One shouted that the other had stolen her husband and she was going to kill her, and this fitted in very nicely and very conveniently with the known facts. Both ghouls faded from view before the atrocious act could be committed.

An article appeared in the press later and the legend of the haunting was born.

Since then various people had claimed to have heard and seen the girls screaming and fighting.

In all probability the whole thing was the concoction of an entrepreneurial landlord who paid the writer handsomely for his efforts, and was rewarded by a substantial increase in business as people flocked from far and wide in the hope of seeing (or at least hearing) the spectres at work.

Dorothea, enterprising as ever, was not prepared to let the issue rest, and revived the story by the simple expedient of pretending to be one of the ghosts. She and little Luce would go upstairs in the wee hours and start screaming in a manner likely to wake the dead, or at the very least disturb the neighbours. And it worked.

After a while the Countryshire Post ran a story which was picked up by the national media and lo and behold business improved appreciably. Several ghost-hunting organisations came and stayed with all their recording equipment but all departed empty-handed, the opposite of Dorothea Dollop whose hands were full of dosh.

She milked it for all she was worth, recounting fictional tales of nights she herself had been disturbed by the ghosts fighting, even embellishing her account on one occasion by saying she had witnessed the dreadful slaying. Financially that did the trick.

So from time to time she and Lucy Hardshaw re-enacted their 'haunting' as before in order to keep the matter alive.

This was all well and good until that fateful night about two years ago.

It was a Thursday night. Arthur had locked up as usual while his wife cleaned the bars and then both had attended to the glasses, leaving everything in reasonably good order for the morning.

Dorothea and Arthur retired to bed, snuggling up together, sharing a joke or two, and were swiftly asleep.

Later Dorothea awoke and was immediately concerned. Then she realised why. Voices were coming from the landing and getting louder and louder. She woke Arthur who was not for waking but who was shaken furiously until he surrendered and came to. The pair of them sat up and heard the squealing which suddenly went silent. Very suddenly. They ventured out onto the landing together to be confronted by a scene they could not readily appreciate. There, before their very eyes, was a figure in white, sufficiently defined to be a young woman, staring at them. They clutched at each other as the figure spoke.

"I am the ghost of Catherine Kinton. I stole my sister's husband and she has just stabbed me to death. Beware Dorothea Dollop. Do you trust your own husband? Because I will steal him as I stole my sister's husband. I am coming for him and nothing can stop me. I will have Arthur for my own, I promise you. And you cannot stab me to death for I am dead already."

And with that she was gone.

Dorothea and Arthur hugged each other. The haunting had come back to haunt them. But the damage was done.

Mrs Dollop kept a very close eye on Mr Dollop from that time forward, and even had he wished to stray there would've been no opportunity. But from his point of view the incident had an advantage, for Dorothea had since been prepared to satisfy his every desire many times over in order to avoid his being stolen away and this suited him perfectly, not to say that it didn't leave him exhausted and in no fit state to dream of pastures anew anyway.

The haunting of the inn was duly relegated, Dorothea telling Lucy that it was for the best that they didn't perform together again for the time being. She watched Arthur like a hawk but continued to satisfy his every lust. Everybody happy.

The Dollops kept their experience to themselves but, of course, never forgot it. The apparition never returned but there was always the worry that she might be back any night, not that it bothered Arthur very much these days. Dorothea or Catherine, might be a difficult choice!

One of the regulars with a season ticket to the private bar was Nathan Grundle, a carpenter by trade, who was sweet on Lucy Hardshaw. He had no time for the stories about the haunting, laughing these off with ease and suggesting, as has been described, they were the creations of the landlords and worthy of nothing more than mockery.

Drinking in the 'privy' as it was known he was making eyes at Lucy who was returning his gaze with interest and winking periodically, such as when he hadn't bought a pint for some while. Tomorrow he was off to the next village down the valley, Much Blather, to do some work for a young widow and was wondering whether he stood the best chance with little Luce or his new client Mrs Crumidge.

Chapter Four

Nathan checked all his tools and packed them in his van ready for departure.

His head throbbed with the hangover from the previous evening's drinking and he hoped he wasn't over the limit for driving. Not that he felt he needed to worry; the long arm of the law was not long enough to reach up the valley and he was only going five miles down the road.

Much Blather was a ten minute drive and waiting for him was widow Crumidge, a comely woman blessed with age and experience, not quite so much of one but plenty of the other.

***

Much Blather

Approaching the village from the north the visitor chances upon a most picturesque scene.

The river swings to the west and Much Blather occupies a sheltered position on the north bank facing the south and the sun. Given the good soil and the advantages of position many residents have developed excellent and colourful gardens which catch the eye almost at once, especially with the background of the valley and the Flemm in the field of vision.

This is one of the oldest inhabited parts of Flemmdale with a few cottages dating back to Tudor times and one or two villagers who look as if they do too. The properties appear to cling together for safety with the lane an afterthought, strung between the houses wheresoever there might be sufficient width for a horse and cart, never mind today's traffic.

It therefore goes without saying that parking is impossible, but a generous farmer donated a substantial part of a field just outside for the purpose and extended his generosity to making parking free (overnight prohibited). This magnanimous gesture may have had something to do with his wife running the popular Hedgerow Tea Rooms which sat between field and village and which was obviously unavoidable to pedestrians. Many partook of meals and refreshments here in the season.

All in all Much Blather was the loveliest of all the dalesland settlements and certainly the most visited on the tourist trail. Nathan had been born here and as such was a Blatherer, so he had known Mrs Crumidge from way back when. He had known her husband Lionel too, until cancer took him in his prime, a blameless individual torn away from family and friends as too many cancer sufferers are. His last two months on earth had been spent in hospital, beyond repair and in desperate pain, finally barely able to speak, his agonising last days a fearsomely inconsolable period for his family.

It was about the time Angelica Crumidge gave up believing in God.

She wasn't a local lass, born and bred in Oddchester, the nearest city. She moved to Much Blather with Lionel when they were wed. Her husband came from Sawe Bottom just a couple of miles away but he'd always dreamed of living here and of bringing his wife to this vision of paradise.

They raised three children, one of each Lionel had always joked, but like so many children of the vale the two girls and the boy had moved away there being so little employment and prospects in Flemmdale.

Nathan parked in the field and walked to her semi-detached cottage with its astoundingly beautiful and well-kept garden which she maintained in Lionel's memory. He would've been so proud.

The carpenter's work today involved erecting a masterpiece in the main bedroom. Angelica had decided to move out all the old furniture and have fitted cupboards instead, Nathan producing various plans and suggestions, and purchasing the necessary materials once the final decision was made. These had been delivered and now he was ready to start.

He politely declined tea and set about his tasks.

A craftsman, everything had to be just so. A perfectionist, he would never bodge something just because it was hidden, never to be seen. He detested the clowns, as he called them, who thought a bent nail was fine if it was behind something and out of view. He'd promised Angelica he'd try and finish in a day but gave himself scope should he need to return tomorrow.

He completed the project with time to spare, pausing only once to partake of a tasty light lunch his hostess had prepared, and on two other brief occasions to answer the call of nature. He'd found her such wonderful company, a very warm-hearted woman, compassionate and full of good conversation that put him totally at ease. He decided he did indeed have a soft spot for her.

To be truthful Angelica was playing to her audience, for she recognised she had ignited some masculine fires and wondered if she might benefit from his interest if she encouraged it and allowed him access all areas, her chief consideration being that he might offer a discount if he was thus satisfied. In that respect Nathan might well have completed the job for free but for the fact it was his living and he needed the money.

Angelica felt if he did have a soft spot for her it was located between his ears.

Mr Grundle left for home about 10.30 p.m., a very happy, contented and satisfied young man. It had taken Mrs Crumidge about twenty minutes to vanquish all his hopes and dreams about Lucy Hardshaw, and her reward had been an appreciable discount. Being a fairly typical male Nathan did not understand Angelica's wiles and cunning ways any more than he understood that Lucy enticed him to ensure he spent as much time and money as possible in the Beau Nidle.

Angelica looked around her perfect bedroom, grateful to the carpenter in more ways than one, for she had enjoyed his company and all the craftsmanship he had demonstrated during his stay. He was truly skilled with all his tools and had satisfied this customer.

She slipped between the sheets, turned out the lights and drifted into a deep sleep. Tomorrow she was going to walk down to Sawe Bottom to spend a little time with Lionel's parents, as was her wont on alternate Thursdays. They had been such lovely in-laws and showed great support when she was widowed, and it was always a welcome diversion to go and have a decent chat with them.

About the time Angelica was falling asleep Caroline Hedge-Rowe was just finishing her cleaning job and looking forward to climbing into bed, another successful day behind her. The farmer's wife had been busy in her tea rooms since opening time and despite the modest description of the premises served an exquisite range of evening meals, popular with visitors and locals alike.

She didn't work single-handed having a small army of locally-recruited helpers who each came in for around five or six hours at a time, and up to about three times a week. Today's assistants were Peggy Dasher, who lived up to her surname and worked like a Trojan, Grace Thumble, who was not built for speed and was thus the opposite of Peggy, and the young Olivia Dimbeaux who was useful and enthusiastic but not very bright. Caroline employed her in a kind of philanthropic way realising the poor girl, through no fault of her own, was unlikely to get a job elsewhere and certainly not in the village.

It was Olivia who accompanied Caroline for the last three hours and who was mainly engaged in collecting up dishes and general cleaning duties as the last diners left and the door was locked at closing time. They had nearly finished when Olivia suddenly burst into tears.

Although she had reared six children Caroline was not maternal by nature and snapped at the miserable Olivia.

"Whazza matter?" Ever the polite young lady Olivia replied between the sobs:

"Oh Mrs Hedge-Rowe, I'm so unhappy, so very unhappy." Caroline relented and came and put an arm around her assistant.

"I know I'm hopeless. I'll never have a proper job Mrs Hedge-Rowe......" and the tears became a torrent as she nestled into Caroline's chest.

Feeling sorry for her Caroline came to a sudden decision.

"Look Olivia, I was going to chat to you at the weekend (she lied) but I'll tell you now. I'm going to offer you a full-time post with immediate effect and (she was thinking on her feet) with the job title Special Assistant." The tears started to dry up.

"Oh really? Oh Mrs Hedge-Rowe, that's so kind of you, but I won't be any good..."

22

"Yes you will. I'm offering this post because I've been watching you and I'm very, veryimpressed and I know you will make a great success of it. Now what do you say to that?"

"Oh I'm so grateful. You've made me very happy. Do you really think I'll be good at it?"

"Of course I do. I'll train you as necessary and make sure you're successful." Olivia smiled at last.

And, thought Caroline, I really will make sure it works, you better believe it young lady, because I can't afford to let you fail. With that she explained the details, that she would work at least five days out of seven and for eight hours a day with breaks of course. She produced a salary off the top of her head, in truth a meagre offering, but saw from Olivia's expression it was very acceptable.

"I'll put the information in writing and you can have it at the weekend." Olivia departed soon after a very happy girl while Caroline breathed a sort of sigh of relief.

A little later she reached her bed where Mr Hedge-Rowe was snoring peacefully and silently extinguished the light and slipped in beside him. I'll tell him about the appointment in the morning when he will probably have kittens as usual, she decided.

She'd learned that it was always best to present her husband with a fait-accompli rather than run an idea past him first, and then to simply withstand any blast that a revelation might create.

A little further up the road an excited Olivia Dimbeaux, wearing an expression of self-satisfaction, had arrived home to be greeted by joyous parents. She had good news that would please them.

"Gor dad, worked a treat, worked a treat, just like you said it would. Cried me bleedin' eyes out an' she went all soft and hugged me and then I cried even harder! You was well right dad. Worked a treat."

"Knew it would. What did I tell you? What did I tell you?" cried a satisfied father.

"Anyway she gives me a full-time job like, and a silly title she thinks I'll be proud of. Daft bitch."

"Go on Livi, what's yer title then?" mum asked eagerly.

"I'm a …… wait for it ….. wait for it ….I'm a Special Assistant!" And all three fell about laughing. "Did just what you told me dad an' sucked 'er in. Kept telling 'er 'ow useless I was like, and she told me I was going to be a great success."

"Well done Livi, me an' yer mum, we're proud of you."

"Yeah, and she thinks I'm the stupid one!"

"Tell you what," mum interjected, "my nan used to have a term for it. She'd have said old Hedge-Rowe was done up like a kipper. Good for you girl. Now make sure you *do* make a success of it."

"Count on it mum, just count on it."

Chapter Five

Shortly after 10 a.m. Angelica Crumidge left home on foot for her in-laws, ignoring the very slight drizzle which, according to the Met Office, should clear up by late morning. What a wonderful evening she'd spent with Nathan. Perhaps she should invite him back for a repeat performance, but then maybe not. Might encourage him, and it might not be so good second time around.

Better to cherish fabulous memories than run the risk of souring them.

She was soon passing the parish church, the only place of worship in Flemmdale, the church where she and Lionel were married, and she spent a few moments recalling that it had become a place of scandal that had amused the whole valley. Wonder what God makes of that, she pondered?

Her thoughts then changed direction as she remembered some gardening she needed to do when she got home later. Her father-in-law would drive her home lunchtime, as he always did, just part of a pleasant and agreeable ritual. And it was as various gardening activities were being sorted through her mind that she came upon Sawe Bottom.

***

Sawe Bottom

The Sawe has a grand title as a river for it is not much more than a large stream.

At the point where it flows into the Flemm a small hamlet had grown up, the Rectory being among the few properties there. All are close to both rivers and some are affected by occasional flooding when the waters rise noticeably after continuous heavy rain in the hills. The Crumidges' pretty cottage sits right on the banks of the Sawe and possesses plenty of sandbags for the owners to protect it, and successfully so thus far.

The Rectory sits back a trifle and has not required sandbag protection just yet.

But flooding is the least of worries for the occupants.

The Rev. Titus Newt, an old-fashioned fire-and-brimstone preacher, has been busy doing God's work and equally busy doing work not likely to appeal to his spiritual boss.

To date he has had a fling with Rectory's cleaner, an affair with the organist and is currently trying his luck with the secretary of the Parochial Church Council. It would appear the recipients of his attentions do not mind attracting the resultant gossip, and have welcomed his interest with open arms.

It might have been supposed that the vicar's wife, Matilda, Tilly to her friends, could be considered a long-suffering victim, worthy of pity and support. But on the basis that what's good for the gander is good for the goose she had embarked on a similar programme to her husband and, to date, had snared a churchwarden, the verger and a Sunday school teacher.

Mr Forester, the churchwarden, appeared to be one of life's gentlemen, always smartly dressed and well-groomed, a man much admired for his good looks and his charming manners. Six feet tall he had the physique of an athlete which only added to his allure where the opposite sex was concerned.

By some contrast Mr Healey, the verger, although younger, was rather over-weight and tubby. Different again was the much younger Davey Jones, the Sunday school teacher, who was of short stature, fairly thin but with an angelic and appealing face.

For Tilly Newt it was indeed a case of all creatures great and small.

Despite behaving in an ungodly fashion with these men Tilly never forgot her devotion to the Good Lord and often cried out 'Oh God, Oh God, Oh God' at the height of her passion.

Being a vicar Titus went a step further, usually kneeling by the bed in silent prayer before blessing himself and his lover, who was inevitably growing impatient, and afterwards praying for the Lord's forgiveness and the redemption of their souls.

Unknown to the dale's gossip-mongers was the actual relationship between the two Newts.

Curiously they seemed to achieve gratification in discussing their extra-marital exploits with each other prior to indulging in the pleasures of the flesh, after which they would join together in singing a hymn or two.

Their union had not produced children, which was perhaps just as well, and Tilly was now beyond child-bearing ability so frequent attempts at procreation were not likely to result in any unpleasant problems.

Titus's favourite was the organist, a middle-aged spinster rejoicing in the name of Felicity Farre whose experience of men was extremely limited, and whose education in the subject was improving rapidly under the vicar's tutorage. An accomplished musician who had a grand piano at home she had grown to love the man's visits, starting each session entertaining him with a short recital of his favourite music, and afterwards accompanying their singing of a hymn.

He nicknamed her Filly Farre and would regale her with silly comments, such as 'how *far* shall go tonight Filly Farre?' which she lapped up and laughed at.

"You're such a tease Titus, but you make me so happy."

His jokes were corny and often stale chestnuts, such as:

"Do you believe in the hereafter Filly?"

"Yes I do Titus."

"Then you'll know what I'm here after…."

The strange thing about all this was that the previously paltry numbers in the congregation actually increased when the stories became common knowledge, and it was never clear whether newcomers were there to praise God or increase the depth of the tittle-tattle that ran amok in the valley.

However, matters did not always run smoothly.

There had been a fearful occasion when Tilly had been entertaining Davey Jones at the Rectory when her husband arrived home unexpectedly with Filly Farre in tow, and they'd had to hide under the bed while Titus and Filly made hay above them and treated them to a subsequent rendition of 'God is working his purpose out as year succeeds to year' bellowing the concluding lines 'When the earth shall be filled with the Glory of God as the waters cover the sea'. A lengthy hymn they thankfully settled for two verses, thankfully for Tilly and Davey.

Nemesis arrived for Titus in the autumn that year. For reasons unaccounted for he developed painful and troublesome

27

haemorrhoids which put paid to his non-religious adventures and which created the foundation for much mirth.

Children would gather outside his home chanting 'The Rector's wrecked his rectum' whilst the editor of the parish magazine couldn't resist a dig writing that Father Newt would be coping with his workload despite having piles to do, and would be getting to the bottom of all of it. Being the vicar of Sawe Bottom was never going to be a help when people were so insensitive.

In the privy at the Beau Nidle Alan Bassett said it was a good job Newt did most of his work on his knees, but in time the humour ran its course and faded just as Titus duly recovered, and with his recovery he resumed his pleasures.

Today, while Angelica Crumidge chatted with her in-laws and Father Newt was away seeing the bishop in Oddchester, Tilly was going for a hat-trick she'd had her heart set on for a long time, namely all three lovers in one day. Albert Forester was first up, to use an expression, and the event was well underway, much to the disgust of Ruben Berry toiling in the garden. He did not approve, and not because he had been ignored in Tilly Newt's less-than-clandestine carnal hunts, but because in his eyes adultery was a sin.

Berry was, depending on your point of view, either a very appropriate name or an unfortunate one for an undertaker, yet that was the profession Ruben had followed until retirement. Now he tended various gardens in the area and this morning he was at the Rectory. Since he had also worked as a gravedigger when such service was required he was used to digging the soil.

Ruben had been born in the next hamlet, Upper Hande, and had returned there, just as he'd dreamed, once retirement came. By good fortune the home where he was born came up for sale just after his 66th birthday and three months later he and his wife Marianne had moved in.

At lunchtime he'd be leaving this den of iniquity, as he believed Sawe Bottom to be, and heading for home and his own garden. He was well known and loved, and was often to be observed pushing his wheelbarrow with all his tools aboard along the country lane one way or the other. He thought it apt that a native of Upper Hande was called a Handeman, and he was proud of the fact too.

Chapter Six

Normally Ruben would knock for his money but he knew Mrs Newt was busy and might not be in a position to answer the door, or have any inclination to do so. He packed his wheelbarrow and made his way out into the lane, crossing the bridge over the Sawe, waving to Mr Crumidge and his daughter-in-law as they drove past in the opposite direction, and set off at a brisk pace for Upper Hande.

He did not dwell long on the sadness he felt about the Newts, miserable sinners who were at least in the right position to seek the Almighty's forgiveness, especially Father Newt who must surely have the next best thing to a hot line to heaven.

His thoughts turned swiftly to his own life and his marriage, a relationship built on pure love, eternal and enduring love, mutual respect, faith and trust. And what a glorious time it had all been. Not that it was devoid of sorrowfulness and tragedy, but that was part of life and something to be accepted.

Ruben paused about halfway on his route where there was a seat dedicated to the memory of 'Doris Herdwick who loved this spot.' He remembered Auntie Doris, as he called her, from his youngest days and today chose to sit on her seat and continue his reverie about his life while gazing down the beautiful Flemm valley.

***

Upper Hande

Ruben and his younger brother Alec had been home births at a time when such occurrences carried extra risk. Both were under five when their parents moved to a semi on the outskirts of Great Barsterd so that their children might be better placed for education and employment purposes, but the move was not welcomed by the boys who loved their cottage and the countryside and were loathed to leave it.

The lack of chances to play outside, and the lack of venues appertaining to such adventure, soon led the boisterous Alec into trouble, and trouble followed him to school. The much quieter and more studious Ruben enjoyed school and, having passed the eleven-plus, was later accommodated at the Great Barsterd Grammar whereas Alec ended up at the Comprehensive and on the road to ruin.

Although Ruben obtained eight GCE O-levels and then five A-levels he turned down the thought of further education or possibly university due to an extraordinary set of circumstances that led him into his career.

Within the space of three years all four much-loved grandparents passed away and Ruben became fascinated by funerals. There were two burials and two cremations. In the case of his maternal grandfather the ashes were later scattered at sea, the lovely gentleman having been a sailor and in the merchant navy during the war.

He somehow survived the freezing waters when his ship was torpedoed while on the Kola Run, the Arctic convoys to northern Russia. He had been on a return trip before, an icy hell of a dangerous operation, where unbelievable coldness and extreme weather conditions conspired with the enemy to cheapen life having made it unbearable first. You could be attacked from the air, from below the surface and above it, and then there had been the threat of Germany's great capital ships such as the Scharnhorst and the Tirpitz. And if your ship sank there was simply the unforgiving sea to finish you off.

At least at that temperature the end could be swift. Ruben's grandad had been rescued by a warship almost at once but he had suffered terribly from his bitter immersion. He was lucky. Quite often the warships couldn't help – they had to keep moving.

Leaving school armed with all his GCEs Ruben disappointed his parents by applying for a post at the local undertakers. Shock horror! But his parents had their hands full elsewhere.

Alec left school without a qualification to soil his abysmal record, obtained work in a local record shop and fell in with all the wrong people. This was the Swinging Sixties, the time of the Beatles and the Stones, and Alec was determined to swing.

It was at the undertakers that Ruben met Marianne, the receptionist at the time. Both were shy and reserved and it was months before he drummed up the courage to ask her out. He took her to the pictures, a coffee bar afterwards and took great care to get her home before nine-thirty as decreed by her father. Another eight weeks passed before they shared a kiss. It was a Saturday afternoon and they were walking in the park. He purchased ice creams and they strolled around the duck pond her free hand held firmly in his while they ate their treats. Then they wandered towards the trees, their refreshments finished, and there they stopped to gaze into each other's eyes. In that moment nothing else existed, nothing else mattered.

"M-M-M-Marianne," he stammered, "please may I .... may I .... kiss you?" There was no reply for none was needed. He gently slid his arms around her waist and she nestled to him as their lips met. It wasn't passionate, it was more juvenile, the kiss of the nervous and inexperienced, for neither had kissed anyone before. But it was beautiful and it spoke a million words of love.

A couple of months further on Ruben and Marianne visited her father where her suitor politely did the right thing and asked for his daughter's hand in marriage, a request that was granted at once, subject to certain provisions primarily relating to his career prospects and how they would find a home. Being practical people they had already looked into the latter issue.

He was making a success of being an undertaker and there was every chance of him becoming a partner. The weird irony of this, however, was that the firm would then be known as "De'Ath, Berry and Burns" as the senior partner was Harry De'Ath and the junior Richard Burns. How they had ever made such an amazing success of De'Ath and Burns was impossible to gauge, but it was perhaps in spite of the name rather than because of it.

In time Ruben married his blushing bride on a sopping wet summer Saturday and their honeymoon was spent at the Royal Hotel in Prattle, just three nights, all they could afford, and then they moved into their Victorian terrace two-up, two-down to begin life together. Their wedding night was a voyage of exploration and discovery, as lovely as it was romantic, made all the more beautiful by being the first time they had experienced intimacy.

Until then they had made do with kisses and cuddles. Fully clothed.

In time Ruben did indeed become a partner and De'Ath, Berry and Burns went from strength to strength.

The Berry's had two children, two fine girls, and eventually were able to afford a better property in a more salubrious part of an ever-growing town.

The hammer-blows came one after the other. Marianne's father died suddenly, shortly before they fished Alec's body out of the river. He'd fallen in while drunk. His mother never got over it and she became unwell and was taken from them two years hence. The saddest of times for Ruben and Marianne.

But there were many happy times, such as when their eldest daughter Chloe graduated which made them the proudest parents in creation. Unfortunately, degree in hand, she secured an appointment with an American company which meant spending most of her time in the USA. Since Ruben and Marianne had never held passports they only see her when she makes fleeting trips back home, but they are nonetheless joyous occasions.

Younger daughter Francesca had a brief career in advertising before marrying and becoming a full-time mum, presenting the Berry's with five grandchildren.

Marianne's mother and Ruben's father became close friends sharing the warmth of good company, but there was never anything beyond that. The undertakers business was eventually sold to new owners, Messers Goffin and Deadman, hardly giving the concern an improved name.

Ruben's daydream was interrupted by Oliver Buckett going past in his empty minibus and he suddenly realised, looking at his watch, he'd be late for lunch, not that Marianne would really mind. Approaching home he waved to a neighbour, Judith Birke, who was just pulling into her drive. She worked all kinds of hours at a Great Barsterd supermarket and lived with her mother Noreen.

Both had been unlucky in love. Noreen had been deserted by her brutal husband when Judith was fourteen and the girl herself, an only child, saw her engagement ended when her fiancé punched her in the face, telling her it was what she deserved and he'd got another girl. Mother and daughter swore they would have nothing to do with men at all after that.

But Judith, now thirty-five, was experiencing something else and was unable to establish what it was she was feeling, and why. Yes, she'd loved Malcolm dearly until he broke two teeth and her heart in one foul move. Yet the sensations she was getting now were similar to the feelings she'd had for Malcolm but, thankfully, there was obviously no man in sight.

It was a puzzle.

What she didn't realise was that a young woman she often worked with, and had become a close friend, had developed a great affection for Judith, an affection in danger of growing deeper, and she was unintentionally making her affection clear with her glances alone. Ms Birke enjoyed Tamsin Hare's company greatly yet was incapable of comprehending the signals being emitted.

Tamsin was a frequent visitor to Upper Hande where she was made welcome. Noreen felt she was like the sister Judith never had but had become conscious of her interest in her daughter and decided it was best not to talk about it.

A cat proved to be the catalyst for improving the relationship between the girls and along the lines Tamsin was daring to wish for. Hoping against hope, it has to be said, for her love was a secret love, a love never to be declared unless Judith showed signs of response. She couldn't take the chance of ruining a treasured friendship and perhaps never being with Judith again. It was unthinkable. Best to suffer the pain and anguish, the almost unbearable anguish, and enjoy their times together, and cry herself to sleep at night alone in her bed.

Noreen had adopted a rescue cat she named Kitcat which slept most of the day and slipped off into the countryside at night on unknown feline adventures. Kitcat, a delightful marmalade, lapped up the attention the Birkes gave her and rewarded them for their kindness by periodically bringing home a mouse or other small creature as a gift, unaware humans have no culinary use for such items.

On this particular day the girls were sitting on the sofa chatting while Noreen worked in the kitchen garden. Kitcat strolled in and leaped into Judith's lap whereupon she was caressed just the way she liked, her eyes closing with apparent pleasure. Seeing Tamsin smiling and studying the happy cat Judith asked a question she might've phrased differently had she thought about it.

"Here Tam, would you like to stroke my pussy?" Tamsin burst into spontaneous laughter and her friend joined in once she realised what she'd said, going bright red into the bargain. Tamsin took a chance hoping her effort would be dismissed as part of the humour of the moment if Judith took it the wrong way.

"Oh what an offer Jude! How could a girl refuse? If I stroke yours how about you stroke mine?"

"You haven't got a cat Tam." There was an awkward pause in the laughter, and Tamsin swallowed hard, curling her bottom lip under the top, anxiety and despair suddenly etched in her face.

"I know. Sorry, it was a joke," she stuttered. But they were now looking directly into each others' eyes, Judith finally awake to the girl's intentions and equally awake, at long last, to the feelings she had herself, now able to identifying those warm, tender feelings within that had made no sense until now.

Kitcat was ignored and jumped to the floor displeased her pleasures had come to a premature end. Tamsin leaned forward wishing lady luck was smiling upon her and was rewarded when Judith closed the gap between them and their lips met in an explosion of happiness and desire.

They briefly parted but the truth was upon them and surrendering to the irrestsible force they both felt they grabbed each other and caressed each other furiously, passionately as their lips again melted together with equal fervour. Kitcat looked at them sporting a look that might have said 'and this is what my cuddle was given up for?'

The cat wandered off knowing there were no further comforts to be looked forward to right now.

It took Noreen a little while to get used to the relationship but in the end she accepted that everyone was their own person and should be free to love whomsoever they pleased. Love can arrive unbid, an unstoppable and compelling force, no matter who you are. Why allow anything, especially old entrenched ideas, to get in the way? After all her lovely daughter was happier than ever, but would she lose her now and have to live alone with only Kitcat for company?

Thankfully not. With her agreement Tamsin gave up her rented flat in Great Barsterd and moved in with them at Upper Hande, an arrangement that suited them all, especially the cat.

"Here mum." Judith announced one day, "Just thought. Our surnames. Me and Tamsin. We're Birke and Hare!" Mum shared their laughter as she shared their joy and as she shared their lives, a contented trio. Well, quartet if you include the cat.

Chapter Seven

Noreen had a part-time job at a florist's in the next village, Sharpe Corner, and today being Friday she was on her cycle pedalling the three and a half miles to her destination.

Well, it was a florist after a fashion, but in truth it sold many other things including newspapers, confectionery, wool and knitting patterns, greetings cards and so on. It had taken the place of the unviable village store which closed a few years back, but did not sell groceries or the range of products the store once did.

There was a small outdoor section for the florist was also a garden centre yet one poorly stocked other than for compost of which it held copious quantities all year round.

Sharpe Corner was a large village with a mixture of buildings old and new including a small close of so-called affordable housing that had sprung up a couple of years ago. Residents thought it odd that getting planning permission out here in the country was extremely difficult but when the Council wanted to be seen 'doing its bit' a handful of allegedly affordable properties could be approved without a problem.

***

Sharpe Corner

The Florist was Miss Deborah Gumboot who was unwed but not from choice. She had a sweet round face with long blonde hair that was usually tied up in a bun. Her smile could dissolve anger at twelve paces, disarm the most aggressive person, and make the most depressed and unhappy soul feel elated again.

She tended towards being full-bodied but at six feet tall that might appear to have been more of an asset and an important salient feature in attracting a mate. Long, shapely legs enhanced and completed the picture. But of Mr Right there was no sign.

There had been little sign of mister anybody.

So Deborah took the lead and went a-hunting. Perhaps she didn't have the right techniques for she failed more than she succeeded. She took a gentleman she fancied in High Stayckes a large and very beautiful bouquet of flowers, but whilst he appreciated the gesture and adored the blooms when he had decanted them into vases and placed them around his home, he thought it an odd gesture. Not a gift most men would value maybe.

Since he also thought he was the victim of a PR promotion for the florist the operation was doomed from the outset. Although she took his photo while he was holding the bouquet in an embarrassed manner it was for her mantlepiece and not for advertising purposes.

She tried to woo a man named Paul Syde in Great Barsterd but he was having none of it. For one thing, being about five feet four inches tall he felt she almost towered over him, noticeably when her hair was tied in the bun. Poor Deborah had even tried using that hair to her advantage, once saying to a man she'd been chatting to in Sawe Bottom:

"Would you like to see all my hair spread over a pillow? Your pillow." She was all smoulder and sizzle, her eyes afire with raw desire, her facial expression a come-to-bed invitation.

"Well, been nice talking to you. Must dash." The simple response.

But was she downhearted? Never! To offset the disappointments there had been some uplifting times.

Up at Much Blather she had been bedded by Willie Bostle, an ugly but very keen male specimen. To paraphrase a masculine term, she decided, there was no need to look at the stoker while he's getting the fire going. She thought Willie was very thick, but she was being complimentary and not speaking about his mind.

Miss Gumboot made eyes at a male customer in her shop who returned her gaze with interest added, and then asked her for a date. Everything was arranged but then she discovered he was married and she was having none of that, date cancelled.

She had lively experience with a Darren Bumbridge from somewhere or other, a man she described as having a wicked tongue, again being complimentary. It transpired he was a businessman visiting the area, looking for a quick fix which Deborah unwittingly provided, and then he was gone together with his five-star tongue.

This morning, as soon as Noreen arrived, Deborah was away on deliveries, white van lady on the road. First to drop off some pre-ordered affordable cyclamen to an affordable couple in the affordable housing in Nora Bone Close, thence to Little Pryck with six sacks of compost for one address and two bags for another. At Nether Noing she fulfilled a telephoned order for just one bag plus some weed-and-feed for the lawn, some weed killer, a large fork and a spade.

She rang the bell and the door was opened by a dream of a man.

"Mm ... Mm ... Mr Longcastle?" she enquired, stammering as the nerves overtook her.

"Why yes, that's me. Are you Miss Gumboot the florist?"

"I am sir," she replied, regaining a little composure and confidence, "and I've brought what you ordered. If you tell me where you'd like them I'll unload and then you can check them over. If there's anything you'd rather not have I'll take it back and obviously you won't be charged."

His smile was destroying all her defences, not that she'd left many standing once she'd set eyes on him.

"Just by the side gate here will be fine, and I'll give you a hand. Do please call me Simon."

"Oh ... yes ... fine ... thanks .... and I'm Bedorah, I mean Deborah."

"Thanks for delivering this Deborah. Let's get this stuff in." Which is what they did. He continued,

"I'm sure you're very busy but if you'd like a drink, well, the kettle's just boiled."

Deborah was not so busy she'd turn down such a hunk of a man. 'Spect he's married, she thought, so she tested the water.

"That's kind, er Simon. Hope Mrs Longcastle won't mind."

"I'm not married and nobody on my horizon."

Whoopee she thought as her heartbeat raced on ahead of her. I'll have a coffee and take your time making it, like all day.

"I'd love a coffee please Simon."

"Black or white? Sugar?"

"White please, just a little milk and no sugar thanks."

She sat at the kitchen table as bid and throbbed uncontrollably.

"Please forgive me," he requested, "but I called you Miss Gumboot. Are you Mrs or do you prefer Ms?"

"Miss for me Simon. Unmarried and nobody on my horizon either," she giggled.

"How interesting," he observed. Hoped it would be she thought. He brought the drinks to the table, offered a biscuit which was declined, and sat down close to her.

"You've not been here long Simon?"

"Nope, bought the place about two months ago. I expect the old bush-telegraph works well in the country here ......" He was smiling in a delightfully knowing way and she coyly returned his grin, acknowledging that, yes, you can't keep things quiet out in the wilds.

"May I ask what you do Simon?"

"Yes of course. I own four rather diverse businesses in and around Great Barsterd. There's the garage and mini-store on Fulchest Road (she nodded her knowledge of the place), the Homes-a-go-go estate agency on the High Street (that was a surprise), which is how I came to find this place (she slightly raised her eyebrows), Castle Metals over on the industrial estate in Nickersdown Way, that's scrap metal, non-ferrous we deal in (she made a mmmm sound, trying to appear educated when she didn't actually know what non-ferrous meant), and then, for my sins, I own Undie Paradise, the ladies lingerie shop, also on the High Street. (Deborah almost gurgled into her coffee mug as her eyes opened wide. She'd bought some very racy underwear there only two weeks ago).

"I know, I know," he continued, with a broad grin decorating his face and his hands held up in a kind of gesture of mock surrender, "what am I doing in ladies underwear? Well, I bought the place from the lady who set it all up, Mrs Poddle, do you know her? (Deborah shook her head). I think she was having a bad year trade-wise and then the poor lady's husband passed away. I know very little about ladies lingerie but I have an excellent manager who is running the business very well. Harriet Wimsure, do you know her?"

"Yes, I know Harriet as an acquaintance, and I do shop there Simon. In fact I think I'm wearing a pair of your knickers now … Oh … Oh …. silly me, that must sound awful." And she guffawed in a very uneasy yet ladylike manner while he laughed gently and kindly sensing her embarrassment.

"Not at all Deborah, and I'm pleased to know you're a customer," he responded, softly patting her hand where it rested on the table. The touch alone was enough to send her to seventh heaven. The look on his handsome face turned her to jelly in a most pleasant way, a way she had never experienced before, and she was longing for him to try the dessert he'd just created.

"You must be a very clever man Simon," she asked when she had pulled some of herself together.

"Dear me no. I've been lucky ……"

"You may have been lucky some of the time Simon," she interrupted, "but you are clearly an entrepreneur and a shrewd man of business and I admire you."

"That's as may be, but I suspect you are a successful businesswoman Deborah, and you must have a thriving concern there. How did it all start?"

She pulled her chair closer to the table to be nearer to the man, and spoke in a quiet almost conspiratorial whisper so that he had to lean forward to hear her.

Inadvertently gabbling nineteen to the dozen in her anxious state she told him how her mother had run the shop as a florist, but when Deborah was old enough to join her it became all too clear such a facility was never going to work in a small village. So she'd persuaded mum to diversify and when the village store closed she added some of the services the store had provided, and now the whole affair ran quite profitably, even employing some part-time help.

"Goodness me Deborah, you're an entrepreneur yourself," he exclaimed as she swooned and fluttered her eyelids involuntarily.

"Not as good as you Simon……"

"Much better Deborah, much better than I."

"Oo … get away with you….."

"No, I really mean that. I assume mum's looking after base right now?"

"I lost mum just a few months ago Simon."

"Deborah, Deborah, I am so sorry, and it must be so painful for you. It was rather thoughtless of me. Please forgive me."

"Simon, please, you couldn't have known, but yes, it's still raw," and she felt the tears rise as she fought to control them lest they should fall. Her failure to do so was not her fault. Sensing her distress Simon rose quietly and put a consoling arm around her shoulders and hugged her to him. She allowed herself to be drawn into his comforting breast and with that the tears made good their escape and poured forth while she sobbed profusely. He hugged her all the more.

In time she improved permitting his comforting to wash all over her and warm her.

"I lost dad when I was eight," she added when she felt better, "so there's just me. No brothers or sisters." His response was softly spoken.

"Then we are both orphans, neither of us with siblings either." The realisation swept over her as the words sank in.

"Oh Simon, I'm so sorry."

"Yes, my own mother passed away three years ago, a grand lady, and my dear old dad died after a serious accident at work five years ago."

She looked up him and pursed her tear-sodden lips.

"Yes, it would seem we are both orphans as you say."

"Orphans and entrepreneurs Deborah." His beautiful smile lit up her entire world, her whole life and she knew then she wanted him desperately, and wanted him forever and longer. He hunkered down so his face was close to hers, his expression one of compassion and tenderness, and she could not stop herself.

She swivelled in the chair, put her arms around him and kissed him, little more than a peck on the lips but it was enough. Both rose, embraced and then shared a fervent kiss of much more substance. Gawd, Deborah thought soon afterwards, and I've only known him a few minutes! To be precise they had been kissing for nearly a quarter of an hour, and that was on top of unloading the van and then sitting down for a coffee. More like twenty minutes, but probably the most wonderful and glorious twenty minutes she'd spent with any man.

If there is such a thing as love at first sight this was it.

"I think the chemistry thing has overtaken us," he said, confirming her view of love at first sight. His smile was reaching right into her heart and she knew it would not let go. His voice was her own private angelic choir singing songs of sublime love, his arms embraced her soul and would keep her safe and happy to eternity. What temporarily brought an end to the magic was her mobile ringing. It was Noreen with a query. The assistant also asked how long she'd be.

Ending the call it was Simon who spoke first.

"Business eh? Same for both of us orphans and entrepreneurs." They both laughed. "May I take you out to dinner one evening Deborah?"

Yes please, she thought, take me around the stars, do such enchanting things to me, but never ever let me go.

"Well, that's very kind of you Simon. I'm free most nights."

"How about tonight then?" That's the right answer she decided silently.

"That's good for me, but, and I hope you won't mind me mentioning it, I'm afraid I like British if you know what I mean. Sorry if you prefer something exotic, but it isn't me. Hope that's okay."

"My sentiments exactly. There's a lovely riverside restaurant near Thropley, the White Swan. I'll see if I can book a table and we can have a romantic candlelit dinner. We'll go by taxi then we can enjoy some wine together … oh sorry … I'm assuming you like wine."

The White Swan, Thropley. Second mortgage country for Deborah. Very swish. Perhaps, she pondered, he fancies his chances and, do you know what, he has every chance!

"I love wine."

"Good. I'll book the table and collect you about seven-thirty?"

"Yes, that'll be fine. I'd better look out some decent clothes."

"I'm sure you'll look terrific, but please be sure to wear some of my knickers!"

They dissolved into laughter but then it was time to get back to work. She floated out to the van after a lingering farewell kiss and drove back to the shop on a cloud.

Simon Longcastle sat down in an armchair, utterly beguiled. Could this really be the one? She was the finest creature on earth in his opinion, the most beautiful girl he'd ever held in his arms. Loveliness personified. Could this be the one at long last? Time would tell. No other girlfriend had lasted any distance, his heart had been broken too often, but there was something about Deborah he couldn't put his finger on, something so wondrous that set her apart from the others.

He booked the table and the taxi and sat back in the armchair once more. He found himself wondering what sort of knickers she was wearing, for Undie Paradise carried a vast stock. But he let the thought amuse him for a moment only. After all, his sole interest was as a tradesman.....

They shared a most romantic evening at the White Swan, returning to her home about ten.

"Won't you come in for a nightcap Simon?" she asked hopefully, heart in mouth.

"Yes, I'd love to Deborah, if it's not too late for you."

"No, no, I'm often up late but tonight's been so special I want it to go on for ever anyway."

"What a lovely thought my pet. I'll pay the taxi and join you at once."

My pet, my pet, my pet .... She played the words over and over while he was gone and while she adjusted the lighting in the lounge as best she could. Dimmed, but not too dark. Without dimmer switches the process was a challenge but she swiftly found the right combination of table lamps to end up with 'subdued lighting' as she saw it.

She led him into the lounge where he behaved like the imperfect gentleman and swept her bodily up into his arms (what a strong man, she concluded) and sat on the sofa with a compliant Deborah in his lap. Fiery and furious kisses followed, the chances of a nightcap slipping away into the far distance. Their cuddles and caresses matched the fervour of their wild passionate kisses.

And it came to pass that, about eleven twenty that evening, Simon found out exactly what knickers Deborah was wearing.

Chapter Eight

Despite spending the last few hours in paradise with the god of her choosing, it didn't alter the fact it was Saturday morning and Deborah was up early to take in and sort the papers. She did have a willing pair of extra hands to assist her. Simon was only too pleased to help.

He'd had the night of his life and was already fretting, unnecessarily, about losing the girl of his dreams that had suddenly walked into his life. He needn't have worried. There was no chance of losing Deborah. She was as hooked as he was.

They were both yawning widely when Mrs Crombie came in to help, freeing Deborah to run Simon home in her van. Sadly she had to return immediately so no chance of breakfast together, but they agreed to meet the next day and enjoy a peaceful walk in Flemmdale.

As they drove out of Sharpe Corner they passed Oliver's mini-bus and its solitary passenger going the other way. The passenger wasn't going much further, just to the next hamlet, Bordham Witlass.

***

Bordham Witlass

Emmeline Munch wasn't the only passenger, the other one being out of sight on the floor. Her faithful Collie bearing the name Fetchit went everywhere with her.

An octogenarian, she lived with Fetchit at Little Pryck, and travelled to Bordham Witlass to collect her pension at the post office. She did not have a bus pass and paid her fare in cash determined to ensure her details never appeared on any computer.

"You'll never find me on one of those damned computers," she'd once told Oliver, "as they are the instrument of the devil himself." Oliver had smiled to himself knowing full well she was on more computer bases than she could ever imagine. Local council and state pension just for starters!

She also had no time for men. She could think of no reason why such horrible, useless creatures should exist at all, and felt that women could get by comfortably without them. Obviously she had not stopped to wonder how her mother had given birth to nine children, possibly believing pregnancy was a simple act of nature that occurred anyway.

Emmeline was born in a disgusting hovel in Oddchester before the second world war. It was soon after the Depression but her father was lucky to have work on the railways where he was a fireman. It had probably not occurred to her that her papa was a useful male since his work produced the only income they had and they all had to live on it.

She was the sixth child and now she had outlived all her siblings. Her father died in the war; although he was in a reserved occupation firing the engines he was sadly a victim of a bombing raid which destroyed much of a depot, his locomotive included.

Gradually the family's fortunes improved, Emmeline herself taking on employment as a maid, and soon after the war they were able to move into better accommodation. In time, as the need for maids decreased, she became a live-in companion to an old housebound lady, and then continued in service as a lady-who-does, doing domestic cleaning work and other duties. When she retired she and her mother decamped the big city and headed for the hills and the fresh air, finding a decent cottage in Little Pryck that was entirely to their liking, and there they stayed until her mama passed away a few years ago. Thinking she might like to return to what she called civilisation Emmeline looked at urban properties in Great Barsterd, but soon discovered the town wasn't worth a light and remained at the cottage and acquired a dog for good measure.

Fetchit proved a successful hound when it came being good company and a good guard dog, but had a propensity for finding things before they were lost. On one occasion, when the pair were out for a walk in the valley, Fetchit sprinted for a small thicket on some pretext or other, disappeared for a few seconds, whereupon there was a feminine squeal and a masculine cry of "get off", and the dog promptly came racing back with a pair of knickers and a pair of pants in its mouth.

Woman and dog now made their way into the Post Office.

That the PO survived at all in such a tiny hamlet in this day and age was down to two things. It was the only one in the valley and there was a public outcry when closure was proposed, and it was also a book shop that sold a few pharmaceutical items as well, a hardware store, a pet and horse supplies centre, and a farm shop which ensured its viability.

The Postmistress, Penelope Podium, watched Miss Munch and Fetchit approach the counter, knowing what the answer to her first question would be.

"How much Miss Munch?"

"All of it."

Her pension was counted and handed over, Emmeline moving on to the book department. The assistant there, Jackie Crumpton, took a step back and spoke.

"Don't come too near Miss Munch, I've got the snivellums."

"Snivellums? What's they?"

"Well I'm sniffing and sneezing and probably got a cold coming."

"Get that tin of liniment over there and rub your chest. It's big enough."

"My chest?"

"The tin."

Jackie took another step back.

"Besides missy you shouldn't be at work if you're not healthy." Jackie ignored her by changing the subject.

"Oh, we've got the latest Maggie Hope in. Would you like a copy?"

"Yes please, but tell me where, don't want your germs."

She was directed accordingly. Miss Crumpton had often wondered why a woman who didn't think men needed to exist at all found pleasure reading what were, to some degree, romantic novels. Maybe they reflected a love long lost, or perhaps the books had taken the place of men in Miss Munch's life.

Having made her purchase which included two other paperbacks Emmeline brought Fetchit round to the pet section. She enquired of the dog whether he wanted this or that, bought

47

what she believed the collie had approved, and headed for the farm shop.

The owner of the entire emporium, Douglas Mintpick, was there to greet her.

"Lovely to see you again, Miss Munch. Hope you're well."

"Reasonably well disposed Mr Mintpick, and Fetchit is fine as you can see. But Miss Crumpton shouldn't be here; she's sick."

"Thank you Miss Munch, I'll send her home shortly." And with that busied himself sorting some potatoes out.

Having bought some eggs and vegetables and a bottle of apple juice purporting to come from Flemmdale (she knew of no orchard or individual apple trees) she asked Mr Mintpick if he knew what time Oliver Buckett would be back from Great Barsterd. They had this conversation every time. Since nobody knew what Mr Buckett was up to and where it was a pointless question.

But there was purpose to the request.

"Don't worry Miss Munch, I'll drive you home in the van when you're ready."

"Thank you Mr Mintpick, that's so kind."

There, he thought, I'm another useful male. See?

Miss Munch's views on the opposite sex were well known everywhere. The dialogue about the mini-bus cropped up every visit and always had the same result, a lift home for Emmeline and Fetchit.

Today, by chance, there was a variation.

Mr Mintpick put her purchases safely in the back of his van while she climbed into the passenger seat, then he held the back door open for the dog. But Fetchit barked twice, suddenly scampered across the road and leaped a stone wall.

"Ye gods," cried Douglas, "what's got into him?"

"What's happened? What's up Mr Mintpick?"

"Miss Munch, I'm sorry but Fetchit has just shot off over that wall there," he explained pointing in a vague direction. Emmeline muttered and accepted assistance back out of the van and began calling. Barks could be heard in the distance but of Fetchit there was no sign.

The two humans went over to the wall and called out but all they received were barks in reply. Then Fetchit appeared close to the river bank barking some more. But he would not come back despite his owner calling him a naughty boy who wouldn't get any treats later.

"What are we to do Miss Munch?" a despairing Douglas Mintpick asked. Just then Jackie Crumpton appeared on the scene enduring a particularly hearty attack of the snivellums.

"Ish trine t' tell ush sumshing," she cried through her hanky. Mintpick was good at translating snivellage into English. He explained to an exasperated Emmeline.

"Jackie says he's trying to tell us something. I think she means we need to go to him rather than get him to come to us." Jackie was nodding furiously.

"Well, one of you go then. Whatever next." Upon this matronly command Jackie looked at Douglas and he at her and Jackie decided she'd just been elected to carry out the task.

"Take my mobile Jackie. Just in case." He handed his phone over and a cold feeling flowed through her. He's had a premonition, she reasoned, and grabbed the mobile, climbed over a gate and dashed across the field towards Fetchit taking her snivellums with her.

Girl and dog vanished.

Then Penelope Podium came trotting out full of disorder.

"Douglas, it's Jackie on the phone. There's a young child down there, fallen in the river, numb with the cold and wet, and she's trapped under a branch and she's in danger of drowning."

"Tell her I'm coming and call an ambulance Penny. Grab some blankets, towels, anything like that and put the kettle on, and start a fire somewhere." With that he climbed the gate, caught his foot and fell headlong into the field.

"Oh f-f-f-f-f...."

"*Mister Mintpick*, please, there's no need for language," cried a shocked Emmeline, "and do get a move on." He picked himself up and did as he was bid.

By the time he'd reached the riverside Jackie, up to her waist in the water, was supporting the sobbing girl and keeping her safe. Douglas weighed up the situation and hurling himself into the river managed to move the branch that was causing the trouble and Jackie was able to lift her onto the bank.

He took the child in his arms and ran up towards the post office, passing her over the wall to Penny Podium who wrapped her in blankets and took her to the rear office where Jake Throwby, seconded from the pet shop, had lit the wood burner.

The women looked after the stricken, frightened girl and were able to extract her name and address but not her phone number. Douglas recognised both surname and address, checked his customer list and phoned her parents in Sawe Bottom. They arrived about the same time as the paramedic and about ten minutes before the ambulance.

Katy, for that was her name, recovered her spirits and went to hospital for a check-up where she was pronounced to in perfect working order and was taken home by her parents.

The eight-year-old been playing with two friends but they had lost her and she had walked for miles down the riverside until, exhausted, she fell in. Weakened, she could only make pitiful noises but Fetchit had heard them.

Needless to say Fetchit was the toast of Flemmdale and promised a medal by the grateful parents. He seemed much happier with the doggy-chews they bought him. Jackie's immersion appeared to have cured her snivellums, or at least they were easily forgotten. She and Douglas were hailed as the human heroes but, being self-effacing they said it was all down to the dog, which up to a point was completely true.

Eventually, having changed his soaking wet clothes and dried himself, Douglas was able to take Emmeline home. Outside her abode she turned to him and spoke.

"Mr Mintpick. You were wonderful. You got everything organised as you shot off to the rescue and not only did you do well saving her, you came flying back with her so the ladies could tend her. Then you notified her parents. I must say, Mr Mintpick, you are a credit to your sex, and I have never had cause to say that to any man. A credit, Mr Mintpick, a credit."

He sat back with a smile on his face. Coming from Emmeline Munch they were quite the most special words he could've heard. He took the shopping to her door, as well as a bag of doggy-goodies that everyone present had chipped in for, and then they both stood aside as a guard of honour as the true hero trotted up the path and into his home to a round of applause.

Well done Fetchit!

Chapter Nine

Interlude

The Flemm valley, land of legend, drama, beauty, of rugged hillsides and soft verdant pastures, of timeless serenity and delightful countryside, of people and animals and history

The Romans and Normans, and most other invaders for that matter, did not waste time in the dale, and tarried but briefly.

The Normans did build a motte-and-bailey castle with a wooden keep at the place now known as Great Barsterd but there is nothing to mark the spot now, the exact location lying under a supermarket.

History suggests the valley had been sparsely populated until just over two hundred and fifty years ago when numbers increased, the odd cottage dotted here and there suddenly finding themselves with neighbours as the hamlets and villages developed. Gregarious things, properties, but additional housing appears to have been as unwelcome then as now.

From the middle ages onwards wool meant wealth here as in many parts of the country, and the rich merchants built their grand houses in Barsterd, adding the prefix Great to emphasise their importance and building a large, elaborate church to help demonstrate their prosperity.

There seems to have been little industry here otherwise, with no evidence of minerals being found in these hills, and even the industrial revolution failed to encourage activity in that direction. The wool merchants did not respond to mechanisation and suffered for it, the town following suit fairly quickly, going into rapid decline. The railways came and went, the town's station surviving just eighty years, perishing before the second world war.

But the valley watched all these happenings from a safe distance and made no effort to change itself. It tolerated the intrusion of more human beings because it had no choice, but it kept an eye on them nonetheless.

The source of the river Flemm is a small lake (more of a pond really) that is fed by water running down the upper reaches of the hills. It is thought the lake sits quietly in a volcanic hollow surrounded by rock, the ideal conduit for channelling the waters. At first it tumbles and splutters, bubbles and swishes as it takes its first steps towards the distant dale, its youthful frenzy taking it hither and thither until that fervour is spent and it calms itself into a free-flowing waterway.

Various tributaries come and join in the fun, but eventually the Flemm widens and slows and becomes a grand and elegant lady, processing steadily down the loveliest part of a picturesque vale, magnanimously accepting waters from further sources, such as the river Sawe, and progressing at its own pace for Great Barsterd and beyond.

Occasionally heavy rain or melting snow create a stronger, more powerful river that gathers pace and fury and causes damage to lands, to banks and to nearby properties. But mostly this is a benign medium for the movement of water, and one that cruises gently onwards, through less undulating countryside, through Oddchester and thence to the sea, many miles away.

***

The legend of the twin sisters

A story handed down by generations is a tale relating to twin sisters Matilda and Eleanor Shrubb who lived in a remote cottage not far from Sawe Bottom in the seventeenth century.

It was hard to tell them apart and they were inclined to play on this for their amusement and to the consternation of others.

But there was one strange difference, an oddity amongst twins.

Matilda wished to be wed and longed for love and the feel of a man, whereas Eleanor had no such desires, hoping no man would ever come for her. Their parents wanted them both wed (and off their hands if truth be told) and the father frequently

53

made enquiries when he met other local folk. But the valley at that time did not seem to be home to any eligible males.

Their father kept a small herd of cows and was assisted by an older man called Grendle Warmlet who had always rather liked the look of the girls ever since they had come of age, and had secretly harboured an interest in marrying one, despite his advanced years. Matilda or Eleanor, either would do.

Eventually he approached their father to test the lie of the land. Conscious of Eleanor's aversion Mr Shrubb proposed that daughter on two grounds. Mr Warmlet was unlikely to bother her very much given his age, so that should suit her, and secondly he would be relieved of a problem of what to do with her as her own years advanced. Mr Shrubb had another reason: He'd found a husband for Matilda at long last so shipping them both out about the same time had great appeal.

Poor Eleanor's reluctance was only slightly eased by the knowledge that Grendle Warmlet probably required little more than a companion and a woman to carry out all the womanly chores about the house.

Mr Shrubb, with the agreement of the bridegrooms, arranged a double wedding and Matilda could hardly wait, bursting at the seams with excitement and showing scant sympathy for her sister. However, the girls, mischievous to the last, decided they would dress the same and just for fun take each others' place at the altar, easily changing places after the ceremony.

Unfortunately the best laid plans can go astray.

Immediately after the wedding Grendle lifted Eleanor (actually Matilda) up into his arms and took her to his pony and trap, setting off for the hills without a second thought. A horrified Matilda (actually Eleanor) stared in terror at Edward Godbit (for that was his name) and recoiled at the look of lust in his eyes, her worst nightmares personified.

After partaking of some hospitality with Mr and Mrs Shrubb Edward took Eleanor's arm and escorted the fearful, shaking girl to his horse which they rode together to his humble abode further down the valley. He had no idea he had the wrong twin, anymore than Grendle realised. But the girls were victims of their own folly and there was no way out.

However, the story appeared to have a happy outcome, for Eleanor discovered the joys of being married to a well-endowed young stud and gave birth to seven children, one after the other. Matilda, initially disappointed, soon learned that her husband's procreational appurtenance, although the same age as its owner, was surprisingly large and proved wholly satisfying, Grendle's enthusiasm for pleasure equalling that of his wife. They had six children before Grendle expired. The cause of death is not recorded.

Is there any truth in the story? Well, you must judge for yourself.

***

Great Barsterd

A long, long way from Bordham Witlass, where we temporarily halted on our journey down the valley, lies the market town of Great Barsterd of which you will have read much already.

Four bridges cross the Flemm and a pleasant riverside walk has been created thanks to funding from the EU. That didn't stop the overwhelming majority of residents voting for Brexit. The town boasts two of the major supermarkets and a surprisingly vibrant and successful High Street area where business thrives in the main.

Nowadays industry is varied and there is plenty of employment. Tourism has become an essential feature with the Flemm valley a major attraction, and two medium size hotels have appeared together with a number of B&Bs and the old established Queens Hotel, a former coaching inn, weighing in as far as accommodation is concerned.

There is a mixture of housing from new developments to the older terraced rows, from pleasant suburban semis to the detached properties only the wealthy can afford. There has been the suggestion of reinstating the rail link to Oddchester but it seems unlikely to come to fruit. Many who live here work in Oddchester but the car reigns supreme although there is also an excellent bus service too.

Great Barsterd has proved an attraction for the young of Flemmdale, there being so little employment opportunity up the valley. The town is indeed reborn after its demise in the nineteenth century. It has a football club whose ambitions exceed the ability of the manager and the players, an amateur cricket club of reasonable repute, and two golf clubs where ladies are reluctantly accepted but have proved themselves the equal of men.

The market is held twice a week and is a far cry from the markets of old. Once you could've come here to barter for sheep and cows, to buy meat and vegetables, but now it is all mainly about the drivers of unmarked white vans flogging handbags, cheap gaudy clothes and horrible jewellery.

***

The tale of the infamous Mayor of Great Barsterd and the milkmaid

In the late nineteenth century a very proud, pompous, arrogant and hypocritical man became Mayor of Great Barsterd, and you'd have thought he'd been crowned supreme ruler of the universe.

It was the general consensus among the people that he had made a reasonable proportion of his money in nefarious ways with blackmail high on the list. It was certainly agreed that he had probably wangled the post by twisting the arms of fellow councillors by fair means or foul.

Folk believed that he might yet face a day of reckoning here on earth although most assumed he would have to wait until he stood before the Good Lord on the day of judgment, with his next destination likely to be down rather than up with the angels. As it happened he was brought to book, and with a loud and very public bang, by a very humble medium, and during his mayoralty.

The Mayor's name was William Dolleigh Fyne-Pratt, and you are welcome to make of that what you will as you will only be following in the footsteps of the residents at the time, most of whom detested the man and joked about him behind his back.

His first task, upon appointment, was to commission a statue of himself to be placed outside the town hall, and another in the market square. Both erections were destined to have short lives.

WDFP as he became known strutted around in his chain of office fully expecting people to bow and curtsey to him, although few did, and he set about making life a misery for all and sundry, little realising they were mocking him in his absence. A rotund gentleman, much given to sweating and most definitely not given to walking far, he used the mayoral coach and horses for even the shortest of official journeys, and some unofficial ones as well.

His wife, Gertrude, was of similar build and was just as pompous, determined to enjoy his year in office. They made a ridiculous pair and were routinely laughed at.

"There go a pair of Pratts," the Chief Treasurer whispered to the Chief Clerk as they witnessed the two being driven away to open the new library.

"Aye," replied the Chief Clerk, "a jolly fine Dolleigh Fyne Pratt!"

Needless to say the Mayor was guest of honour at the Flemmdale Agricultural Fair, a show dating back centuries. He was asked to judge the best bull and set about his task with no knowledge whatsoever of what he was looking for. A mischievous farmer, forewarned that the Mayor would be given the task, displayed a cow and persuaded his milkmaid, the comely Clara, to present the beast.

There was much lip-smacking and hilarity in anticipation, yet most believed even a complete idiot like Fyne-Pratt must surely see through the ruse straight away. But they hadn't reckoned on the role Clara was to play.

Eagerly she warmed to the undertaking, making sure she looked absolutely alluring in her milk- maids 'uniform' which she had tailored to suit the occasion so that is showed off her best features in a more revealing way. Miss Clara Muggins had an advantage being a tall and very well-proportioned young lady who would've looked exciting and desirable in sack-cloth.

They gave the cow a good-sounding pedigree name, Brutus Asinus Stercus the Third, and trusted the Mayor knew no Latin. And then Clara stood by the cow and waited.

Meanwhile Fyne-Pratt had been expounding his views on farming in a way that demonstrated beyond all reasonable doubt that he had no knowledge of the subject whatsoever. Then it was time for the bulls. He looked at the first three in the line, made some pointless comments about leather and beef, patted the animals all round and looked into their eyes.

"Y'can tell a lot about a bull from its eyes," he informed his audience, speaking with great confidence and oblivious to the chuckles all around him. The next in line was Brutus and Clara and she performed the most gracious and subservient curtsey ensuring that the Mayor would be able to see right down her cleavage and take in most of the hillsides that rose either side of such a deep valley. He was clearly impressed.

Clara spoke garrulously of the animal's pedigree, making it up as she went along, and also ensured the Mayor's attention was on her own assets as he inspected Brutus. But there came the awful moment when he paused and looked down at the cow's well-filled udders. Clara felt the game might be up. What could she do? Metaphorically taking the bull by the horns she decided on a two-prong attack as the best line of defence.

"Y'honour," she said, executing another curtsey, "it is not well known yet but farmer has developed this bull to improve the efficiency of taking the bull to the cows, if you understand me sir. It is a secret and farmer knows he can rely on your discretion. This way the bull can be put in a field of cows and do the entire job in a few hours rather than days. Brutus has a large supply of … well …. you know ….. and a number of …. well … you know … rather than just the one. Very efficient sir." And she curtsied again.

The Mayor looked impressed, unaware he was being taken for a fool.

Clara had played her part magnificently but she still had the second prong of her attack to help keep his mind off the udders.

"I would be only too pleased, y'honour, to show my gratitude in any way you required, should Brutus win," she whispered, leaning forward and displaying her own udders.

"If you are going to be so accommodating, m'dear, I'm certain Brutus has a good chance."

"I vow I will be accommodating sir, you may count upon it."

Game, set and match.

Brutus won first prize with honours and the farmer was praised for his innovative work in the Mayor's speech without revealing the 'secret' he was talking about. The guffawing was deafening and Fyne-Pratt hoped they weren't laughing at him. A vain hope.

Later that day Clara Muggins led the Mayor into a deserted corner and prepared to be accommodating while Fyne-Pratt slipped his trousers and underwear down, unaware he was being secretly photographed. The cameraman was hiding in some bushes waiting to catch him in a compromising position and didn't have long to wait. The exposure was taken, exposure being the operative word, without Fyne-Pratt's knowledge, and the well satisfied Mayor returned to the show and his wife unaware ridicule was just around the corner.

Nemesis, when it came, was a double-whammy.

The local newspaper had pictures of prize-winning Brutus, whose real name was revealed as Daisy, and of William Dolleigh Fyne-Pratt in-flagrante with Clara the milkmaid. The story told how Clara hoodwinked the Mayor and gave a detailed account of the farmer's 'new development' in bovine reproduction! The whole affair soon reached the national press.

Now a complete laughing-stock he was forced to resign in disgrace and his downfall was nearly total. His business interests suffered and he moved to another part of the country and tried to be absolutely anonymous, and failed. Miss Muggins became something of a celebrity and eventually married into wealth and status, a legend in her own lifetime, and her story is told to this day up and down the valley and in Great Barsterd.

**

Tourism

Given the beauty of the area it is no surprise that it attracts visitors all year round.

Cyclists like the winding lanes, inclines and steeper slopes that test their skills and sharpen their fitness, but they are not always the most considerate of road users much to the despair of local people trying to get around.

But then the same can be true of motorists when they are a hindrance to residents of Flemmdale. In the summer the tourists can indeed be a hazard to folk going about the simple task of living their daily lives in the area.

However, some residents, such as the Dollops at the Beau Nidle pub and Mrs Hedge-Rowe at the Hedgerow Tea Rooms, have capitalised. There is a wealth of footpaths criss-crossing the valley, many leading up onto the hills, a good number leading even further afield, so the opportunity for walking is seized with glee, not just by holidaymakers but by day-trippers from the towns and cities and, of course, the locals themselves.

It's a doggy paradise too. If the legends of the haunted inn, of the twin sisters and of the Mayor and the milkmaid belong to earlier eras then the legend of Fetchit's heroics is about the take root.

And it's time now to return to the site of Fetchit's life-saving antics and head on further down the valley. It's Monday and Douglas Mintpick has a delivery to make at the next village, Scrotum-cum-Impubis.

Chapter Ten

Douglas Mintpick loaded his van with hay bales to take to Nunto Stables just outside Scrotum-cum-Impubis and was whistling a happy tune as he did so, still revelling in the joy Fetchit had brought them all and delighted Katy was safe and had fully recovered from her terrible ordeal.

He'd played down his own part and heaped praise on Jackie and both had passed the glory onto the collie.

Climbing into the driving seat his whistling changed to singing, a wordless rendition of Kylie Minogue's 'Never too Late' and a rendition that would've left the listener longing for the original in its place. With that he departed Bordham Witlass for the stables.

***

Scrotum-cum-Impubis

The name might suggest the settlement was ancient and of Roman origin, but it was nothing of the sort. It was named by a small group of Cistern monks who came here in the fourteenth century in the hope of finding a peaceful, away-from-it-all retreat where they could spend their time in prayer and contemplation. The whole project was undone by the Abbot himself who clearly had no idea what a vow of celibacy was. Perhaps the Flemm valley was not the ideal choice after all.

The sad troupe departed soon after, their monastery unfounded, leaving behind the name they'd chosen for the hamlet and two young women with child. The Abbot was sorry to go; so many young maidens seeking his blessing, but too many angry fathers after his blood.

The joint-owner of Nunto Stables, Tracey Paiper, is also the joint-owner of Dale View cottage which she runs as a B & B with accommodation for up to six. The other owner is her partner, Peter Piper, and their surnames are often muddled by the

61

unknowing. Peter is owner of Piper Computer Services, based in Great Barsterd.

Tracey and Peter also own the adjacent property, Monks Delight, which is their home and intentionally named thus as it is the exact spot those monks tried to colonise. Dale View is quite separate but has a kitchen where breakfast for guests is prepared. Normally it is hard to get a booking here in the summer months, the venue attracting five-star reviews on TripAdvisor.

The couple come from affluent backgrounds, Tracey's well-heeled parents setting her up in the Stables and Peter using a gift from his father to buy Monks Delight, the latter being an arrangement to avoid paying too much inheritance tax when Reginald Piper pops his clogs. With the success of Nunto Stables and Piper Computer Services, to say nothing of family connections, there was no problem obtaining a loan for the purchase of Dale View as another business venture.

Tracey chose the unusual name, Nunto, to demonstrate her sense of humour, as in 'plenty of monks but none too many nuns'. No doubt the Abbot might have appreciated a nun or two about the place.

It should go without saying that she employs people to do much of the work in both the Stables and in Dale View, as well as having a cleaning lady for Monks Delight. In Dale View breakfast duties are shared between Eva Russell and Stella Knight, both from the hamlet, and cleaning responsibilities are executed by four other ladies all from neighbouring villages. Four teenage girls, also garnered from this part of the valley, work at the stables for the minimum wage but have found happiness amongst the horses and regard their jobs as labours of love.

There is also a male stable-hand, a young man in his early twenties who by some peculiar coincidence bears the surname Abbott. Luke Abbott is Scrotum-cum-Impubis born and bred and is lusted after by the four girls none of whom has secured his interest, but all of whom are working on it.

One of the reasons Master Abbott does not cast glances in their direction is that he has his hands full with his employer and does not intend to place his job in jeopardy by spreading his gifts more evenly about the stables. There have been days when his services have been required up to four or five times, on each occasion he being summoned for 'business consultations'. When he works at weekends there are no such meetings as, of course, Peter is usually home.

Luke has another demand on his amenities.

Eva Russell once caught him and Tracey in full flow, bursting into Monks Delight on some pretext connected with the B & B, and has used the intelligence to ensure she is not sacked and has a decent supply of the attentions of a young man known to the stable girls as 'the stud with the thud'. Eva is fifty-three, remarkably shapely, long-legged, and still very attractive, also possessing an appetite her sixty-two-year-old husband can no longer satisfy.

Tracey goes in fear of Eva, knowing she could spill the beans and wreck everything. Luke does what he's told by both ladies. If he does not obey Eva Peter will be informed and Luke's well-paid job, *very* well-paid job, will be out the window, together with all the enchanting pleasures he savours with Ms Paiper, and he doesn't want to lose either.

His boss is twenty-nine, built like a fabulous beauty queen with the face of a goddess, and appears to be insatiable, but Luke is coping.

Right now the hitherto rather stable arrangement at Nunto Stables is about to become unstable since it must certainly be an unsustainable operation for the long-term, with the unsuspecting agent for the impending disaster being Eva's friend and fellow breakfast chef, Stella Knight.

Being Monday morning Stella is at work but with little to do. The B & B was full Friday and Saturday but only one couple remain and they are having a light, healthy breakfast, so Stella has not been required to cook or even make a slice of toast. Having ascertained that they need no other service she has decided to wander upstairs to investigate a slight noise she can hear emanating from an unused bedroom.

Earlier Eva, not working today, stopped by for a chat and went off to find Luke, an event that aroused not the tiniest suspicion in Stella's mind, there being no reason why it should. But as she crept towards the bedroom she could just make out Eva's voice accompanied by that of Luke's. Obviously, Stella assumed, they were sorting some problem out in which Eva had sought Luke's assistance, so she thought to join them but to her surprise found the door locked.

"Eva, are you in there?" she called.

"Clear off Stella," Eva shrieked, "I'm just coming." These few words produced turmoil and confusion in Stella's mind, for she was offended by Eva's sharp words but comforted that her friend was about to open the door. Perhaps her words weren't intentionally sharp.

However, Eva did not open the door or utter further dialogue. There was a lot of moaning and groaning, it seemed to Stella, followed by little squeals that led the woman to believe Eva was being held against her will and possibly being attacked. She had to act.

With all her might she put her shoulder to the door, thinking it might be too late to go and fetch the master key, and after a couple of thumps gave it everything she'd got and the door flew open to the sound of handles and other bits and pieces falling on the floor.

The guests, having finished their breakfast, were making their way up the stairs when they bore witness to their waitress breaking a door down. They dashed to the doorway and started to take in the astonishing sight before them. Stella was screaming, her hands clutched to her face in shock, the door was hanging off its hinges, Eva was naked and on all fours on the edge of the bed with Luke, also naked, standing behind her, riding crop in hand.

"He looks like a stallion taking a mare," the male guest remarked.

"Don't be filthy," his wife scolded, "and go and fetch Tracey. Quick, quick." Turning to Stella she cried "Oh for pities sakes woman, be quiet. Is he your husband or something?" Stella shook her head and started calming. The woman hadn't finished with her.

"Well then, pull yourself together. Are these guests you've burst in on?" Stella shook her head again. "Well, who are they then?" Looking at the naked pair she added, "And you two can stop that right now and put some clothes on, for heaven's sake." Luke tamely stopped pleasuring Eva, an easy task now all the strength had gone from his wherewithal, and Eva collapsed in a heap face down on the bed, satisfied and annoyed in equal measures, both having clearly arrived where they were going in the moment before Stella intruded.

Stella meekly explained who they were and the woman tutted.

The man returned with Tracey by which time clothing had been replaced to a small degree.

"Luke, you're fired," bellow Ms Paiper.

"Yep," commented the man, "just before you arrived Tracey." His wife threw him such a glance that he retreated back into the hall without another word.

"Tracey, I think we'd better talk about this, don't you?" Eva observed, giving her a kind of saucy wink which was not appreciated.

An infuriated Tracey Paiper knew she was beaten, and her next task was to deal with the guests, hoping damage to the TripAdvisor rating could be avoided and, since the lady had been taking pictures on her phone, avoid becoming a laughing stock on YouTube and social media.

Happily, once in her office, the couple seemed more amused and bemused than anything else, and Tracey's offer to refund all charges was rejected, much to her surprise.

"Wouldn't hear of it," the woman assured her. "We've had a lovely time. It's excellent accommodation in such a beautiful location and we've had all we paid for, including some entertainment this morning! We won't mention that if we leave a review, of course." Tracey breathed a sigh of relief and crossed her fingers. Next stop her staff.

Of course, there was no question of Luke being sacked, nor would Eva be departing her employ, so how to deal with the distressed Stella, that was the question. For the time being Luke was checking out the broken door and had phoned his friend, Nathan Grundle, the carpenter from Little Pryck to ask for assistance, and was rewarded by a visit later in the morning.

The door was fully repaired in the hope Peter Piper, should he ever look there, would see nothing wrong, Luke having applied a lick of paint here and there as required.

Meanwhile, Tracey had confessed to Stella Knight, but only as far as she needed to go, and pleaded with her not to tell Peter.

"That's alright Tracey, it's not as if it was you and Luke. I'd have thought better of Eva, we've been friends for years, but that's the way things seem to be these days, not that I approve. And as for Luke, well, a much older woman. Shocking, he should be with someone his own age."

And the matter appeared closed, Tracey convinced she'd avoided the worst case scenario.

Stella couldn't face Dale View just at the present so she assured Tracey she'd pop in later and clear up the breakfast things and leave the dining room in good order. Ms Paiper was happy with that as she herself was extremely busy, and had been put behind by all the fuss and bother. She was also anxious to wedge in a quick session with Luke during the day as she felt a bit left out.

He was only too happy to oblige.

Mrs Knight was too shattered and upset to do anything other than go home and lie down. She'd been persuaded to overlook the incident and she'd reluctantly agreed knowing her job brought in valuable additional income for her and her husband.

Feeling much better she went back to Dale View in the afternoon to complete her chores and realised Luke was there tidying up after his decorating work.

"Would you like a tea or coffee Luke?" she called up the stairs.

"Yes please Stella, white coffee one sugar please."

Moments later she brought the cup to where Luke was to be found and having put the drink down on a table unwillingly erupted into tears, her whole body shaking violently. Luke stepped over to offer words of comfort.

"Oh Stella I'm so sorry, I expect it's the shock coming out," was all he could manage, but her suffering appeared to worsen so he put a consoling arm around her, only to find her grabbing hold of him and sobbing her heart out into his chest. He gently led her to the bed where they sat and then he comforted her until the pain eased and the tears started to dry.

Gradually she overcame her distress.

"Yes, yes, you're right Luke," she whimpered, "It's the shock coming out." And with that both stood as she took a hanky to her eyes and then blew her nose. He gave her one more reassuring hug, pleased she was recovering, but was taken by surprise when she looked up and suddenly kissed his lips. It was no more than a thank-you gesture but Luke took it the wrong way and kissed her passionately, Stella succumbing to what proved to be a stunning but welcome activity.

In fact she was so overcome with excitement that they kissed in a tight embrace for several minutes. The outcome now was a foregone conclusion, the repaired door being shut first.

In the stable block later Luke was trying to keep his head below the firing line dreading the possibility Tracey Paiper might want a repeat performance, and after three women he was all spent. Older women, he mused, shaking his head, unbelievable!

Stella went home a changed woman and prepared her husband, who had now been cuckolded of course, a delicious dinner which was followed by a pleasant and enjoyable evening. He couldn't understand the transformation but was grateful all the same.

Tomorrow being Tuesday, Mr Knight, a self-employed painter and decorator, was off to the next village, Compton Burgle, to start work on a property in desperate need of some TLC. And in the meantime life at the Stables et al would return to normal, or as near normal as life could ever be there.

Chapter Eleven

Ian Knight had a spacious if fairly old people carrier that doubled as transport for all the paraphernalia a painter and decorator might take with him when on the job.

He double-checked that he'd packed all he needed for this particular job, yawned and stretched for the umpteenth time and clambered into the driver's seat. He felt tired, but it was good tiredness for his wife Stella had been reborn as the lively, anything-goes kitten, as he'd called her in their courting days, and had treated him to a night to remember.

What a night Mr Knight, he said to himself with a smirk as he set about trying to start his motor. A few seconds later and the machine had produced signs of life, and a few seconds after that he pulled out into the lane, past Nunto Stables, down towards Compton Burgle.

***

Compton Burgle

Tuesday for Gilbert Thrunch was much the same as any other day for Gilbert Thrunch.

He didn't get out much these days, save when his nephew Terry Lean took him for a run, and those days were precious few, Terry living about thirty miles away. Kindly neighbours nipped in for a chat and a cuppa from time to time, made sure he had all he needed, got his shopping in and so on, and kept an eye on the lovely old gentleman.

Gilbert was eighty two, a widower for many years, and had moved here from the suburbs of Oddchester when he retired looking forward to happy times ahead with his beloved wife Edie. Those times lasted an all-too-brief three years and four months, poor Edie suffering a stroke and passing away two days later. It came right out of the blue for she was fit and healthy and had no history of any serious medical problems.

Both children attended the funeral. Connie had emigrated to New Zealand with her husband about a decade earlier and Juliette had married a Gambian and consequently emigrated to the Gambia, but a long time before Connie moved. Now Gilbert was alone family-wise. Terry, his sister's boy, was sixty four, divorced, but pretty busy with his own children and grandchildren in his spare time.

Nonetheless both men treasured their occasional times together. Gilbert had spent last Christmas at Terry's feeling quietly envious of the families that visited.

Mr Thrunch believed in right and proper in an old-fashioned way, so having risen, made the bed and shaved, dressed in a suit with a shirt and tie and highly polished shoes prior to preparing a simple breakfast. He recognised Mr Knight's vehicle going past more from noise than appearance and recalled he was going to help renovate Dawn Cottage at the other end of the village.

The renovation was for a young couple who would be moving in. Dawn Cottage had belonged to his good friend Eric Bungle who died last year leaving poor Gilbert bereft again. They were in and out of each others' homes, always enjoying good conversation, putting the world to rights, reminiscing about the past, the so-called good old days, and nattering about this and that and making the most of the company.

Now Eric was gone.

There was a clump in the hall and Gilbert knew his newspaper had arrived, generously delivered by Mrs Sutton who purchased it at the Florist's in Sharpe Corner, and popped it through the letter box on her way to work in Great Barsterd.

He had a comfortable armchair in his lounge that faced out of the wide bay window, and from where he could watch the world go by. He and Eric used to place small bets on what time Oliver Buckett's mini-bus would go past! Some folk had a routine so he was used to so-and-so walking, cycling or driving by at a certain time, and he knew if they were running late!

Others did not adhere to any routine which made them a modicum more interesting in a way, as Gilbert was never sure who might show up, and he wasn't familiar with everyone. The summer months were pleasing in that respect as there were plenty of tourists to add to his collection of passers-by.

He collected his paper and returned to his seat just in time to notice Mrs Cardine going along with young son Tom walking beside her. Both waved to him as they always did. The paper remained unread as there was a little flurry of activity to be observed. Jack Skyver went past at pace (no wave) followed by Donald Drake (no wave), and then Lesley Bitterne strolled by in the other direction giving Gilbert a smile and a mouthed 'morning' to add to her wave.

As time went by he became aware Mrs Prendergast hadn't put in an appearance, not that she always did, but every now and then she took a short morning walk through the village and back, occasionally calling on Gilbert for a cup of tea, a biscuit and a chat. Obviously not today. He took short walks himself, but arthritis was catching up with him and he was nowhere near as mobile as he was even two years ago. Sometimes the pain in his legs could be unbearable.

Mrs Prendergast had all sorts of health problems and had been in and out of hospital over the recent years, joking that there was hardly a part of her they hadn't operated on. A jovial lady of seventy-four, she'd been married and widowed three times and wisely, in her own opinion, decided to call it a day and not marry again.

When it was quiet on the road outside Mr Thrunch took up his daily paper but found he couldn't concentrate. Something was nagging at him, something was amiss.

Then a stranger hove into view, a young man who stopped outside and studied the premises. To Gilbert he looked smart yet there was an unpleasantness about him that Gilbert couldn't put his finger on. The man then stared at Gilbert, who stared back, and appeared to come to a decision which saw him coming up the garden path and knocking at the door.

Leaving the security chain on Gilbert opened the door and made a polite enquiry of the man.

"Good morning. What can I do for you?"

"Come to read your meters, sir." Oh yes, thought Gilbert, a likely story.

"Where's your identification?"

"Sorry sir, left it in me van. Here, let me in, only take a mo."

"Leave at once or I call the police."

"No need for that sir. Only doing me job. I'll go and get my ID."

He was away at speed and Gilbert thought he'd ring the police. He'd read about these tricksters gaining entry to homes to rob people. Using the non-emergency 101 number his was able to relate the tale in due course and was told to ring 999 if he felt threatened or if the man was seen again in the area.

And that set him thinking about his dear friend Mrs Prendergast.

With that he put on his coat and hat, collected up his favourite walking stick and set off in defiance of the pain now wracking his legs and feet and trod the road north in a determined style. At least he could warn her.

He would not have gone walking today with the pain as it was, but as it happened he was prepared to put up with the agony even though the journey took him much longer than it might have done.

On arrival he was at first surprised to see her front door ajar, then horrified at the thought of why. Was that wretched man in there? He knocked, received no answer and cautiously pushed the door open, slowly making his way inside ignoring the pains he was suffering. Just then Mrs Prendergast appeared at the kitchen door.

"Oh Mr Thrunch, lovely to see you, do come in, just making the meter reader a cuppa, would you like one?"

"Where is he?" But at that moment the man came flying down the stairs with a jewel box in one hand and made for the front door. Mrs Prendergast screamed. Gilbert went to grab hold of the thief but was easily pushed aside. As the man turned to make a dash for it Gilbert, with great presence of mind, stuck his walking stick between the man's legs, an action that brought the villain to the ground.

Without a thought he fell on the man and pinned him to the floor, simultaneously asking Mrs Prendergast to dial 999. There was a bit of a struggle but Gilbert held on, some super-strength coming to his aid, and after calling the police Mrs P came over and sat on the man's legs while her saviour held his arms down. He was done for.

When the police arrived the man was found to have some of Mrs Prendergast's cash on him as well as the jewel box. It transpired that she'd taken him at face value and, at his request, gone to make a drink leaving him with the meters under the stairs. As soon as her back was turned he was off to her bedroom.

Praise was heaped on Gilbert Thrunch from all directions, but what he really appreciated more than anything was sitting and having a natter with his hostess, along with a nice cup of tea of course, once the police had left with their catch and their statements. Sitting comfortably his pains eased to the point of being bearable and he had wonderful company to cheer him up.

Mrs Prendergast offered him a lunch, insisted he accepted, and being too much of a gentleman to refuse they were soon tucking into bangers and mash before retiring to their armchairs once more.

"Mr Thrunch, you are my hero. I am so grateful."

"No Mrs Prendergast, I thank you, but I am no hero. Just happened to be in the right place at the right time."

"Oh Mr Thrunch, you are too modest, too modest. But I really do thank you from the bottom of my heart."

"That's very kind, Mrs Prendergast, and if you don't think it very improper of me I should be so pleased if you called me Gilbert."

"Gilbert …. Gilbert …. what a stately and apt name for one of life's real gentlemen, if you'll forgive me saying so. And I am Celia."

"Celia. Please forgive me, but that is surely one of the finest names for such a lovely lady, a true lady if I may say so."

"Oh Gilbert, that was so nice of you. But tell me, what did actually bring you to my door?"

He explained about his visitor and his call to the police, and then they were interrupted by the arrival of PCSO Angela Mingle who had come to check up on the victim. She told them they had knocked at all the properties in the village and three others had found themselves with the thief on their doorsteps, all turning him away, two phoning the police.

"Dear me, Officer, I feel such a fool, and you read about these things, don't you, and never think you'll be so daft."

"You're not daft, Mrs Prendergast. These evil people prey on folk like you. "By the way Officer," Gilbert interjected, "your colleagues were here very quickly. I assume they came from Great Barsterd or were they in the area, do you know?"

"Well Mr Thrunch, they decided to send a car after your initial call was followed rapidly by the two others, three calls being a clear indication attention was needed. What an absolutely wonderful job you did, Mr Thrunch, a true have-a-go hero...."

"Not me, not me. Did what anyone would've done."

"Mr Thrunch ..... Gilbert, no more modesty," Celia interposed with a girlish giggle that Gilbert felt he rather liked.

Angela Mingle left soon after and Gilbert, having so enjoyed himself with Celia, invited her to lunch at his place tomorrow, which she agreed to without much hesitation. Her hero went home about an hour later and it would be nice to say he walked with a spring in his step, but sadly arthritis had ruined his springs and although he was a happy man the pain dogged his every step, and he was pleased to sit down in his own armchair again.

Celia had waved goodbye from her front door.

"Have you heard about Fetchit the dog Gilbert?"

"Why yes Celia. Now there's a hero in my book, along with Mr Mintpick."

"Well in my book, Gilbert, you're as much a hero as Fetchit."

"I regret I wouldn't make a good collie Celia. With my arthritis I wouldn't be able to come when called!"

And they parted with laughter on their lips, and the friendliest of waves, and a new warmth in their hearts. Tuesday had turned out to be a very special day for both of them, and they now revelled in the lovely feelings of friendship that had grown inside them.

Lovely feelings indeed.

Chapter Twelve

Prudence Potts had been one of Celia's neighbours called upon by the thief and closing the door in his face had phoned the police, so she was delighted he'd been apprehended and by one of their own, dear Mr Thrunch.

In a small place like Compton Burgle (appropriate name that, she'd mused ruefully) news spreads with such rapidity that it is almost dizzying in its effect. Prudence had telephoned everyone she knew and promised to visit Maisie Dotes in the morning to chew the cud.

Maisie lived two miles south along the lane in the hamlet of Lower Down. The two women had been school friends, and friends ever since, despite their paths taking divergent courses, Prudence remaining a spinster from choice and Maisie marrying and having six children.

Handily Miss Potts had a car whereas Mrs Dotes didn't, so the former would drive over Wednesday morning for a jolly good chinwag at the latter's, with a view to discussing all the excitement caused by the thief and the heroic efforts of Mr Thrunch.

***

Lower Down

Prudence could hardly wait and her breakfast was barely eaten before she was in her car and away for Lower Down.

Maisie lived in a short row of pretty cottages. To one side of the terrace was another B & B which was not as popular as Dale View but which was usually busy enough during the summer, and at the opposite end of the terrace was a peculiar looking conglomeration of buildings belonging to the brothers Tom and Mike Flowers.

Tom was the motor mechanic and part of the site was dedicated to his calling, boasting a couple of workshops, one of which was fully equipped to carry out MOTs, a pokey little office awash with paperwork, and a small store for parts. Tom's part of the enterprise was well guarded, with gates, a state-of-the-art security system, and a high fence topped with barbed-wire. The man himself was relatively lithe, athletic in build, exuding fitness.

This was in contrast to his brother Mike who ran a butcher's shop, and looked every inch the quintessential vision of a butcher, being portly, hearty and full of good humour, and always wearing the butcher's apron and a straw hat to complete the picture. He cheeked his customers and they loved him for it. The shop also sold the type of groceries, such as tinned food and frozen items the Florist and Mr Mintpick's farm shop didn't.

His home-made pies were the toast of Flemmdale. His sausages were renowned all over Countryshire. At times his shop throbbed with clients, locals and tourists alike, and there were times when there was a queue outside. To help him he had Bobby McQueen (known as Steve for obvious reasons), his own father (who had retired but couldn't give up), and a young couple from the village, Nancy Albright and Willie Darke who were very keen on each other but too shy to proceed.

Mike's wife, Shirley, and his mother also gave a hand when necessary. It was actually Shirley who made most of the famous pies.

After Tom was born his mother longed for a girl but got Mike instead and was so disappointed she dressed him as a girl for a couple of years, an action that earned him his nickname Rosie which had stuck ever since and which he clearly loved. Rosie Flowers was adored everywhere.

In complete contrast Tom was the quiet one, as yet unwed, who went about his business uttering few words and rarely laughing or even smiling. He serviced most of the vehicles in the area and had plenty of work given some of the cars were positively ancient. He'd tried to give up on Ollie's minibus but Mr Buckett looked so heartbroken when Tom informed him that he relented and continued to fight with it, somehow keeping it on the road.

Today, during a lull in early morning trade, Mike was looking at Nancy and Willie who were busy but managing to find time to glance at each other, the glanced-at looking away at once as soon as the glancer's eyes made contact. Gawd, thought Mike, what a pair of virgins. And what names: Albright and Darke. Blimey. He and Shirley had tried from time to time to encourage the pair but realised they were just too shy. If only, Mike had concluded, more young people could be like that!

Neither had any sort of mobile phone. In his spare time Willie walked the dale, while Nancy would set up her easel wherever the fancy took her and start to paint exercising no skill or sense of artistry whatsoever. Mike had even spoken to their parents on the QT but all four had given up hope, exasperated. Indoors Nancy would read books or draw, and Willie would listen to classical music or enjoy a chat with his dad. They couldn't be encouraged to show an interest in anything else.

It was known that, out on his lengthy walks, Willie often bumped into Nancy who would be busy painting, especially along the river, but any dialogue was assumed to be brief and of no consequence.

However, unbeknown to all and sundry, Nancy and Willie were no shy virgins. Far from it. When they met in the valley it was by arrangement, and although much of the dialogue might indeed have been brief and inconsequential, the action was fiery and red hot.

Of course, they could hardly go to their bedrooms in their parents' homes for such pleasures.

And while Mike and co watched out for their coy glances in the shop they were missing what the hands were up to. Nancy had a way of manipulating a large sausage that could bring Willie to the boil, and he in turn could fire up Nancy by very gently squeezing a chicken breast in a suggestive manner.

It was little wonder her paintings were rubbish. They were a cover story. In their bedrooms they would write extensive love letters and surreptitiously hand them over at work. They often snatched a snog in the cold store and it's amazing they didn't defrost all the frozen meat. When the weather was unsuitable for meeting outdoors they contented themselves with writing love notes the length of novels. Or reading the letters they'd recently exchanged.

Willie had a ground sheet and towels in his back pack, and Nancy's painting gear also housed vital equipment for their combined leisure pursuits. Thus was all concealed from a pack of adults who couldn't see past the obvious.

Today, their lunchbreak was going to be rather different. Nancy's father had gone to work and her mother had joined two friends on a shopping raid in Great Barsterd, travelling by taxi. She and Willie were going to share a bed, her bed, for the first time. So excited was she that she suggested to her lover they try and get the afternoon off so they could liberally extend their hour until the likely arrival time of mumsie, possibly around 3 p.m. Asking Mike at different times, and knowing the shop would not be too busy, their efforts were rewarded without Mike considering their requests suspicious.

By a quarter past twelve they were on the bed letting fly.

Now, if the course of true love does not always run smoothly, the course of deception can be stormy, so there was consternation and blind panic when mumsie turned up just after two. They had to make decisions in split seconds and one of the more bizarre ones led to Willie being bundled out of the window onto the flat roof of the conservatory below, his clothes being bundled after him while Nancy hastily dressed indoors.

Her mother was surprised to find her home but accepted her explanation about having the afternoon off as the shop was quiet. Then there was a shriek and a cry of 'Oh bugger' emanating from the garden. The women rushed to the rear where mumsie was treated to the sight of a naked Willie sprawled in her azaleas.

"Oh Willie, Willie," squealed his beloved, who was no more aghast than her mother who threw her hands to her face then screamed 'Oh God' several times. Willie had unbalanced himself trying to dance into his underpants, the difficulties faced by many a man struggling to dress in the morning, and fell off the conservatory breaking his fall on the plants but luckily breaking no bones.

He was led inside, mumsie covering his nether region with a tea-towel, and given medical attention for a few cuts and bruises while Nancy went upstairs to retrieve the rest of his clothes. Once good order was restored it was time for the three of them to sit in the lounge and for the inquest to begin.

But mumsie started by delivering a surprise.

"Look, you're nineteen Nancy, and Willie you're twenty-one. You don't have to hide. I'd rather you didn't go to bed together in my home, but there is no need for deception. I trust you're taking precautions?"

"Yes mum, I'm on the pill."

"Well, thank God for that. It seems just about everybody has been hoping you'd get together. Not least me and your dad, and your parents too Willie. I don't approve, but you must have enough money for a night in a hotel or something. I take it this was the first time?" They both blushed, silently unveiling the truth, which in itself was a lie of course.

"Oh dear me. Well, as long as you've taken precautions at least that's one worry we haven't got. But why the deception?" It was Willie who answered.

"To tell the truth the more people wanted us to be an item the funnier it got. We've just played it along for a laugh, like, but we'd have told you eventually. Just having a laugh Mrs Albright, that was all."

"That was a laugh today wasn't it Willie? You'd have been in stitches alright if you'd hurt yourself badly. You might have had broken bones to contend with, you young fool. And you young lady, I'd have expected better of you. All I ask now is that you both forget to mention it to your father because he won't see the funny side, believe me. Let's just keep mum, eh?" Both nodded.

If Mrs Albright had been given a shock, then up at the garage Tom Flowers was also in for one.

He dreaded seeing Hortense Winders draw up in her Fiesta. A single lady, of very appreciable wealth, she'd bought an old farm house near the village and made a good fist of doing it up tastefully. Or at least her contractors had. She moved in and found herself attracting the attention of young males lacking her financial prosperity. Those she fancied, and frankly that was most of them, she allowed closer inspection of her fifty-seven-year-old body, dumping them as soon as they had given their all.

She knew they were after her money, but she made the most of their efforts, enjoying every moment and lapping up the intimacy, the cat with the cream.

But it was a different matter when it came to trying to land a more permanent fish, and right now Tom Flowers was in her sights. If she'd had asdic it would've been a case of 'instantaneous echo'.

The problem was that she really had no idea how to woo a man and tended to coarseness of expression when addressing Tom, her lecherous leer only adding to the man's dismay and dreariness. Today was no exception.

"Tom, it's about time you got your hands on my big end," followed soon afterwards by "I expect you've got a really firm crankshaft." Her risqué double-entendres were lost on Tom and this afternoon he'd had enough of her. He led her into his office and sat her down unaware her excitement was increasing, or that he was going to seriously disappoint her.

"Hortense, thank you for all the business you give me. It is really appreciated. And you have recommended me and that has brought even more business. I cannot tell you how grateful I am. But, please forgive me, I am going to be blunt with you. There is nothing wrong with your car. You look after it, drive it well and, excuse my self-praise, with my servicing it should need little attention. Anybody can check your tyre pressures, your gardener for example.

"But you are such a good customer I don't really mind how often you call, but I beg you, I plead with you, stop these silly remarks you make. I don't find them amusing and, in my opinion, they belittle a fine lady as I am sure you are......" The words died on his lips as Hortense burst into tears and buried her face in her hands. Such action was wasted as Tom had never been one to react to a woman in tears, and he simply rose and walked out the office, whereupon Miss Winders dried her eyes and sat there looking perplexed. Eventually she stormed out after him and found him underneath a Focus.

"Come out of there this minute Tom, I want to talk to you."

"No you don't, you want to shout at me and tear me to pieces and I'm too busy."

"Come out here Tom, or I'll drag you out by the feet."

"That's assault."

"Fine. You can call the police while I talk to you. But I am not having a conversation with the front of a Ford Focus. I want to talk to you now. Not to shout, not to grumble, but to thank you for your honesty. Perhaps it's what I needed, a verbal spanking."

There was a pause then slowly Tom emerged.

He remained on the ground where he pulled himself into a sitting position and drew up his knees.

"Talk then. You've got two minutes."

"Only need one. I apologise but I thought I was amusing you in a sort of bloke-ish way, the way I imagined you men liked. I'm sorry, but thank you for your honesty, and for not taking any notice of my tears. I deserve far worse for being a stupid woman. At my age I should know better. You've been cruel to be kind and I will come to appreciate it. Well, that's my minute up. I'll be off now." And she turned and headed for her car without a backward glance.

Mmmm, thought Tom, that cost her, but maybe she'll be off my back now. Bloody woman.

At that precise second her car made a horrid metallic noise and came to a sudden halt. Tom walked over and looked down at the driver. She had an air of resignation about her as she glanced at him.

"Now then Miss Winders, sounds bad, would you like me to take a look? If I can't do anything right away I'll run you home." Hortense tried a wan smile, nodded in an almost subservient way and sighed as her eyes searched the ground in front of him.

"Thank you Mr Flowers. We understand each other. That's a very kind gesture. "Not at all Miss Winders. You're one of my best customers after all."

She climbed out of the car, humbled but in a strange way very happy.

Tom's assistant, Barry, helped push the Fiesta into the garage. Then Tom came across to Hortense.

"On reflection, no point looking now and keeping you waiting. I'll drive you home Miss Winders." "Thank you Mr Flowers. Is it serious do you think?"

He paused, deep in thought, then replied.

"Could be your big end needs seeing to........."

Chapter Thirteen

Katrina Pulright and her family lived next door to Maisie Dotes in Lower Down and the fifteen-year-old girl had been off school with little more than a head cold since the start of the week.

Her mother feared there was something her daughter wanted to avoid at school but despite several attempts had failed to gain any insight into any problem Katrina might have.

Thursday arrived and mum couldn't persuade her to return to school but did suggest fresh air would be beneficial knowing full well Katrina would jump at the chance to go to the next village. Amply-en-Dowde was less than a mile away and there was a footpath that ran through a field where alpacas were kept, and the girl loved them. If she went there and was fine then there was nothing to prevent her return to education on Friday, or at least that was Mrs Pulright's line of reasoning.

Ronnie Pulright was Juliet's second husband and she had two grown up children from her first marriage. Katrina was the eldest of the second brood, there being a younger sister Carol and younger brother Martin. Mr Pulright left child-rearing to his wife and only stepped in when absolutely necessary. He'd wanted to take Katrina to task over this latest illness but Juliet had begged him to leave well alone, she'd sort it.

Come Thursday morning, as Ronnie prepared to take Carol and Martin to school en route to his place of employment, he made his position quite clear.

"If she doesn't go back tomorrow," he told Juliet, "I'll be sorting her out, believe me I will." Mrs Pulright dreaded his intervention as such interference customarily made things worse not better if history was to be relied upon.

He drove away and shortly afterwards Katrina set off for the alpacas of Amply-en-Dowde.

***

Amply-en-Dowde

On the edge of the village stood a rather grand looking house surrounded by well-tended gardens. It was the master and it gazed down upon the servants, or in this case the cottages of Amply-en-Dowde, and held sway over them, but it was a long time since any villagers had touched their forelocks in the house's direction.

For the young other gestures seemed more appropriate these days.

The present owner, millionaire businessman Sir Doddery Faux-Parr, had taken its simple mock-Georgian façade and tried to create an art-deco masterpiece and had failed on a grand scale, resulting in much local mockery. Think a mix of Victorian gothic, Regency grandeur and baroque and you might get the sickly picture.

Katrina studied this classic example of how to ruin a house's appearance as she always did when she walked past, not that architecture meant much to her, and pondered the age-old mystery of how money could change people and make them incredibly stupid.

Sir Doddery was big in drains. His main company was 'Roddit Through' and he owned another called 'Nu-Age Sewage'. Vans belonging to Roddit Through were emblazoned with the slogan 'Let us unblock your passage'. His wife, Lady Celine, was half his age and came from Jamaica where he had met her while on holiday some years ago. Katrina had resolved never to marry a man for his money. But that was not the reason for the Faux-Parrs' marriage.

Celine was not only wealthy in her own right, she had a great deal more money than Doddery did. Believe it or not they married for love, pure and simple, and they adored each other, a fact lost on local folk. Villagers shunned the couple who had, quite frankly, made no attempt to either integrate or socialise and were consequently despised in the valley.

But this was the Thursday something strange happened, and it began when, for reasons she was unable to recall later, Katrina Pulright decided on impulse to go to the door of their house to try and befriend Celine. She knew Sir Doddery was not there as his Bentley was not in the drive. She also knew it was a pointless task as the door would probably be opened by a maid or some sort of servant or manager, and that she'd be refused admission. It didn't occur to her that nobody from anywhere in Flemmdale was employed there, for if they had been everyone would've known.

Celine herself answered the door, her face a picture of enchanting beauty, although her long hair fell wherever it pleased. She wore rubber gloves, with a cloth in one hand, a bottle of Domestos in the other. Katrina was startled.

"Hello love," Celine chirruped, "what can I do for you?" Too amazed for words it took some while before Katrina could regain her senses,

"M-m-m .... look ... I'm sorry," she stumbled, "I'm Katrina Pulright from Lower Down and I wanted to introduce myself and be friends." Now it was Celine's turn to look astonished.

"Oh ... right ... well ... look, come in Katrina, I'm Celine, just cleaning the downstairs loo, please forgive. Look, come into the lounge, I'll put these things down and join you. Go in and sit y'self down and I'll be there in a few seconds." Katrina hesitated. Celine continued. "Go on Katrina, it's okay, be right there."

A silenced Katrina obeyed and did so rather gingerly. Celine entered and sat.

"Now then babes," Celine began, "tell me about Katrina." It was some while before the girl found her voice but when she did a resume of Miss Pulright's life ensued at some speed.

"You're Lady Celine, aren't you?" Katrina added nervously when her brief tale was told. Celine laughed but not mockingly.

"I'm just Celine. Forget the Lady bit. Please."

"Why were you cleaning the loo ... er ... Celine?"

"I do the cleaning. My husband gives me a hand when he's here, but he's not very good, and I have to keep an eye on him." More chuckles, none shared by her surprise visitor.

"Don't you have a maid?"

"A maid? You're kidding. What on earth for? I'm capable and I love to be doing something. True, I don't go to work, but I fill my days alright. Do the gardening as well and right now I'm writing a book which will probably never be published, but hey, it's fun. It's a romantic tale, about a young woman who falls in love with a man she can't hope to marry, but they do in the end, that sort of thing. What sort of books do you like Katrina?"

Katrina, now in some awe of her host, and shocked by what she was hearing, said she didn't read much and wasn't sure what sort of books she might like, adding that she did enjoy romantic films but her parents rarely gave her the opportunity to watch any.

"I want to marry for love one day, not for money," she appended to her discourse looking straight at Celine who picked up the signals immediately.

"I married for love, Katrina, not for money. I know people think the opposite, but I have a great deal more capital than my husband, not that it would be fair to go any further, it's a private matter, hope you understand." Katrina was taken aback.

"Oh …. I see …. oh …. right …" she stuttered, not sure if she believed what she had just been told.

The conversation remained a trifle stunted until they turned to music and then they found themselves in perfect harmony. Katrina had to field a phone call from mum who wondered if she was okay and who was then stunned to hear where she was. Celine went on to show her guest some music she'd downloaded, the artistes appearing on what to Katrina appeared a mammoth screen that covered half the lounge wall, the music of Miley Cyrus and Adele being played at brain-damaging decibels.

Wow, thought Katrina, this is livin'. The pair ended up dancing to the throbbing music.

"Not allowed to play mine this loud, like," she admitted when it had all ended, "and we've only got a small screen."

"Room's soundproofed, so they don't hear it outside, well, that's as long as I don't open thewindows! You've really enjoyed it Katrina, I mean, being here and all?"

"Yay, been great Celine."

"Well, you must come again. Fancy a coffee or something?"

Drinks made and served they sat and talked about their families, Celine revealing she'd been able to trace her family line in the Caribbean right back to when they were slaves, probably brought from west Africa although that's where the line ran out, there being no further information.

"Wow, you're descended from slaves! How do you feel about that? There's so much about it, you know, the slave trade at the moment, isn't there?"

"Yes there is, and I welcome the way it's being brought into the open. It should never have happened but it was a different age. Making people aware is right but you can't bury or change the past. It's better now but I still get filthy abuse for the colour of my skin. Makes me feel superior, know what I mean, like I think with my brain not with my testicles." Katrina giggled quietly as she listened.

"Wasn't always like that. Used to hurt, make me cry, but then I got to thinking I was better than them. It's not about the colour of your skin, it's about the people we are, simple as that. But the past happened. People did dreadful things in days gone by. And slavery exists in places to the present time. There's always been white slaves, like there were here after the Norman conquest, and that's a thousand years ago.

"Just think babes, women were once burned to death because people thought they were witches. And then there was hanging, drawing and quartering. King Henry the eighth killed his own wives and got away with it. The important thing is that we learn from history so we don't make the same mistakes again, don't you agree?"

"Guess so, but I'm not really into history. But what's hanging, drawing and quartering?"

Celine explained in polite terms but it still made Katrina feel sick.

"And what's that about Henry the eighth then? Who's he? Killed his wives?"

"Yes, king of England back in the day, had a couple executed I think, cos he wanted to marry someone else. Here, anyway babes, what do you do at school then?" She felt the gaps in the girl's education were showing.

Katrina told her and also explained she was off sick with a light cold, now better, but her host could see there was something deeper and decided to probe. Such was the rapport that had grown between them that Katrina soon opened up.

It quickly came to light Katrina was being bullied by another girl.

"You don't have to put up with it these days babes. Remember the slave trade. Racism isn't consigned to the waste bin and neither is slavery, but there's progress. Bullying's the same. Still there but you don't have to endure it my lovely. Tell this girl she'll have me to deal with if she has a go at you again! Seriously, tell y'mum babes. Do it. She can contact the school and sort it. You don't want to be missing school, you just don't."

Katrina was far from convinced but had formed a bond with Lady Faux Parr and therefore resolved she would indeed speak to her mother later.

"You and the family got anything on this Saturday?"

"No, nothing special."

"Great. Doddery's away and I'd love some company. All of you come down here and have a snack. I'll prepare a few tasty treats, love cooking babes, and we'll have a good time, promise. Pleased you're going to talk to mum, but most of all get back to school and get some education into you!"

It was a very different Miss Pulright who returned home later and did as she'd been advised. Juliet was straight onto the school and was asked to call the next day to speak with the Head.

Katrina went back on Friday and her mother and the Head got the ball rolling, and soon the question of bullying was overcome. It was the day Katrina Pulright got her life back on track, and the following day she and her family came over to Amply-en-Dowde and made an adventure out of visiting Celine, a glorious afternoon of fun for all six present, topped with a five-star buffet home-made by the host.

Carol and Martin played in the gardens, they all sat and laughed at a short comedy film on the large screen (volume turned down), and there was no end of agreeable conversation.

In time the Pulrights' returned the compliment and invited the Faux-Parrs' to dinner and initiated the start of a new friendship and the blossoming of the couples' more outgoing approach to living in the country. Soon they were part-and-parcel of the community in Amply-en-Dowde and equally well-known in Lower Down.

And all because an inquisitive bullied teenage schoolgirl took a chance and knocked on someone's door.

About the time Katrina called on Celine another resident of Amply-en-Dowde was trying to overcome a problem.

Suzanne Phillet worked as what is euphemistically called an escort. Born and bred in the village she took over Nook Cottage from her parents when they moved to Birking Witter, a small town the other side of Great Barsterd, to be near their other two daughters and their young families.

Time with the grandchildren was the main attraction and they knew their eldest, Suzanne, was never going to present them with such opportunities.

It's probably fair to say that Suzanne practised procreation with far, far greater frequency than her sisters Etty and Davina but with the object of producing cash not offspring.

Inevitably she was known at school as Fishy-Phillet so perhaps it was equally inevitable she should end up as a hooker. By the time she reached the fifth form she was lusted after by every boy at the Grammar, not that any of them managed to sample the goods, and she attracted even more attention as she went on to take her A-levels, passing maths, English Language, human biology (a useful asset in later life as it turned out) and English Literature.

With that she went to work selling used cars and making a packet from commission on sales. Suzanne knew little about cars, cared even less, but knew how the men operated when confronted by one of the finest examples of sex-on-legs, and consequently could achieve sales with consummate ease. She rented a flat in town and in her spare time entertained punters there, her career being thus born. When her parents wanted to move she was able to obtain a mortgage to buy them out and she returned to Amply-en-Dowde.

Eventually she gave up selling cars. After all, in that profession she had to declare all her earnings to the tax man, whereas she now declared what she fancied and therefore paid little income tax.

Her trade name was Sexy Susie XXX and she was known in her village as Susie the Floozie. Most of her money came from outcalls (i.e. visiting clients in their homes or hotels etc.) but she did a few incalls at Nook Cottage, locally called Nooky Cottage for clear reasons. And it was one such incall booking that was giving her a headache right now.

The customer had the unfortunate name of John Thomas, so he always referred to himself as Jack. He'd first booked Suzanne some months previously and since then had become a frequent-flyer, virtually a season ticket holder, calling on her two, three, occasionally four times a week. He was a pleasure to deal with. A little older than Suzanne he behaved impeccably as a gentleman should, was always clean and fresh and well presented, and treated her with great respect.

There had been some evenings when they had just sat and talked, loving each others' company, and he had paid the agreed rate for her time. She looked forward to his visits but had started to feel guilty about taking his money.

Jack had become a master craftsman making bespoke furniture and now ran a small business dedicated to producing top-quality items to order. For her birthday a few weeks ago he handmade a small coffee table for her lounge and tied a pretty pink bow on one of the beautifully carved legs. The gift had reduced her to tears.

She'd looked into him and found him to be truthful, especially about being single. He was clearly dedicated to his work, and just as dedicated, so it would seem, to spending all his excess cash on Suzanne as he appeared to have no other interests. His only other indulgence was his Merc. She'd also learned that he was tremendously shy and self-effacing and probably never had a girlfriend being too coy to ask one out, although he had spoken of a girl he loved in his teens, a relationship that didn't last the test of time.

Jack's first visit to Nook Cottage had been an experience, Suzanne recalled. Painfully shy, nervous, stuttering his words, shaking a little, he was new to the world of escorts, and new to the world of the opposite sex by all accounts. She'd guided him gently if a little impatiently at first, but made sure he had an experience to remember. She had her ratings to maintain, 4.5 stars overall, and Jack gave her five, adding in his review it had been like being in the arms of a goddess in heaven itself, the perfect girlfriend experience.

And now she was in love with him.

It wasn't against the rules, and not even truly frowned upon, or indeed discouraged, nor was it unheard of in her profession, just rare. A working-girl in love with a punter.

The conundrum for Suzanne was firstly that she didn't imagine for one second that he loved her and secondly even if he did he would not want a partner who bedded other men for a living. He was a self-made, successful and moderately wealthy business man, an artist with incredible abilities, a person who could see such beauty in his magnificent creations, a person who could recognise beauty and rejoice in it.

Had he not praised Flemmdale in positively poetic terms to her?

How could he see beauty in an old hag, as she believed he would see her, one who had been with more men than the grand old duke of York of the rhyme?

She could always go back to selling cars, but it was her history, and for that matter her present, that was against her. Declare her love and he might rock with uncontrollable laughter, call her a silly cow; but no, he wouldn't say anything like that, yet he might say she was a foolish girl and that would hurt just as much.

Perhaps say nothing. In any case he might tire of her soon or find a new escort. Or she could speak her mind and take the results, good or bad.

Jack was due at eight that evening, her only booking today. In the finish she decided to play it by ear, wait until he was there and with no rehearsed words weigh up the situation when they were face-to-face and speak the words that came to her then. It would be the right way to do it.

He parked in the driveway at three minutes to eight and came over and rang the doorbell. Suzanne had been surreptitiously watching from an upstairs window, her heart in her mouth, her whole being throbbing, her mind aching, knowing he might turn tail and she'd never see him again. Whatever, she would take no more money from him, that she'd resolved.

Opening the door his smile melted her sore heart on the spot and she struggled to keep the tears at bay as the agony struck her and stormed her body.

"Come in, come in." She hoped her smile was welcoming and not giving the game away.

"Thank you Suzanne," he responded as he stepped forward. He'd used her real name since she disclosed it weeks and weeks ago, telling her how lovely it was and how it suited her exquisiteness. They went into lounge and sat while Jack produced the envelope with the money, three-hours-worth tonight. She declined, nervously saying he'd earned a freebie.

"Are you cold Suzanne, you seem to be shivering?"

God no, not shivering, she thought, just a bag or nerves dreading what might happen.

"No I'm fine thank you Jack." But he had heard the shakiness in her voice and knew all was not well.

"Something's amiss. I know you too well Suzanne," and he smiled knowingly, his finest and most endearing smile, "but if it's a private matter I'll not intrude."

She tried to control the mass of feelings running amok in her mind and her body and began to wonder if she was even capable of speech. His smile, his most beautiful face, full of concern, full of warmth, all were conspiring to wreck that control and she knew the tears would fall, and her lines of defence would fall with them. As if suddenly becoming aware of her torture he moved swiftly to her side and put an arm around her, and that undid her. She had no choice but to let the words rip from her mouth at any speed they wished and the tears could take care of themselves. Her hands were wringing in her lap and she kept her eyes on them, head bowed.

"Jack, Jack, I love you. I've fallen in love with you. I can't help it," the words plummeted from her lips at high velocity, "I love you, I want you, and I can't help it, it's simply happened and I know it shouldn't, I couldn't stop it, I couldn't. I love you and that's all there is to it……" And the tears overtook her speech. He gave her a barely discernible hug and spoke quietly.

"I love you too, Suzanne. With all my heart. And I couldn't help it either. And I want you too."

And when she turned her head she saw he was crying as well.

"I love you Suzanne. I knew I could never tell you because of your profession, and I'm only a paying client, and I thought you'd laugh at me and send me packing. So I've put up with the pain, the horrible pain. I've gone through agonies every visit when my time with you is nearly up, and suffered terribly when I've driven away. I just want to be with you and love you."

They hugged and hugged, and wept and wept.

Jack had to depart early next morning going home to shave and change for work, but Suzanne made sure he went with a decent breakfast inside him. That evening she would stay at his place and he'd prepare dinner.

She knew she would give up her work, not that he'd said anything, and she had the impression he would let her continue if she wished to, but she did not. She could not hurt him so. Not now. She cancelled the handful of bookings remaining, citing ill-health, and closed her online web account removing all her tantalising details from public gaze. Suzanne was in love and was loved and she would never be a prostitute again.

The delightful coffee table caught her eye and she knelt down and kissed it. It possessed all Jack's love in that sweet moment and she wanted to savour it, for it was a thing of beauty and, of course, quite unique, a most treasured gift.

Would she be selling used cars again? Who knew, but if she returned to her original line of employment she might have a customer almost next door, for Ernie Umpkin's old banger was in its dotage.

It had stirred into life about the time she was dressing and trying to decide what to do with her life this quite magical Friday. Ernie was a window-cleaner and, this being an 'alternate' Friday, his round was due to start in the next village, Evelyn's Hole.

(footnote: please see the Author's Afterthoughts at the end of the book where there is an item relating to some of the views of Celine Faux-Parr)

Chapter Fourteen

Ernie Umpkin checked his ladders were secure on the roofrack and set off for Evelyn's Hole some five miles away.

This is a very pretty stretch of road, offering a slight meander, and journeying between tall trees that look so colourful in autumn, especially on a sunny day with a blue sky backdrop. The road is fairly level and, had he been looking, Ernie would've seen the wide Flemm to his left less than fifty yards away. But he was too familiar with the area to take any notice, least of all on his way to work.

Bunger's Brook cascades down the hills to Ernie's right, a noticeably sharp rising hillside, the brook dropping into a hole in the rocks near the road, to emerge closer to the Flemm which it then joins. In the 17th century there was one house here, belonging to a cobbler Aloysius Dunnet and his wife Evelyn, the latter dipping a bucket into the hole, a natural well, to collect fresh water whenever it was needed.

The spot became known as Evelyn's Hole and the village that developed here took the name.

***

Evelyn's Hole

Mr Umpkin had two clients in the village.

An elderly couple, Mr and Mrs Poleshaw, had lived there for three years, a pension cash-in enhancing their chance to move to the country just a relatively short distance up the Flemm valley where they remained in easy contact with family and not far from civilisation.

They bought a house there because of its position, a picturesque corner with a reasonable sized garden that went right round the property and featured a large pond. There was nothing they liked more than going out and feeding the ducks who lived and bred there, especially when there were new ducklings to be seen.

92

There had been an unfortunate episode soon after they moved when Mrs Poleshaw fell in but was rescued by her husband. Happily the water wasn't that deep.

With much hilarity they decided they would name their home after the incident and a small sign was erected on the gate proclaiming this was "A good duckin'". Whatever the humour and the novelty of the name they innocently chose, they stayed blissfully unaware about how it read on their full address, i.e. 'A good duckin', Evelyn's Hole'.

Ernie's other call was at a bungalow named San Miguel in honour of the occupants' favourite tipple. Richard 'Dickie' Thickwood and Maxwell Forrest had escaped to the country a few years back and done so with mixed feelings which still haunted them. Had they done the right thing?

Well, they seemed happy enough. Dickie was an interior designer and Max an accountant, but perhaps surprisingly it was Max who was the imaginative and creative one in their lives, Dickie the more conservative and cautious half of their relationship. This Friday both were off work at the start of a long weekend where some DIY was on the menu.

Now you might be forgiven for thinking Dickie would be an ace when it came to planning internal alterations but it was Max who proposed the development, drew up some details, costed the scheme and with persuasive words encouraged his partner to proceed.

A skip had been delivered and parked in the drive. With an accountant's attention to detail they had all the materials and equipment to hand. They were ready. Ish.

Dickie had got the day off to a good start by breaking a teacup over breakfast.

"Hope that's not an omen," Max commented, supporting his remark with a rueful grin.

Having checked the Met Office weather forecast they'd decided to bring the furniture out of the lounge, through the conservatory and onto the patio. The previous evening they'd taken all the moveable and breakable objects, the pictures, lights and other paraphernalia to the spare bedroom. Now, one by one, they removed the armchairs, the settee, the dining table and chairs and placed them all on the patio whereupon it started to rain.

With rather more haste they brought the furniture back in. The through-lounge was the object of their DIY so they piled some of the stuff up in the conservatory, smashing a pane of glass in the process, although neither man was sure how and neither accepted any blame. The dining chairs went in the kitchen and the table in the bathroom where it proved an obstacle and a hazard when the toilet was required.

Max cellotaped a plastic bag over the broken window.

The settee was in front of the doors through which they'd planned to bring their equipment from the garage, so that had to be re-sited. Having completed the task and opened the sliding doors they paused to look at the downpour that had overtaken them and which would mean them getting soaked. But it had to be done.

The weaknesses in the non-existent planning were beginning to become manifest. The lounge was being given a make-over and although the destination was clear the route was uncharted. Consequently the pair simply brought all their gear from the garage and sited it in the room in no particular order. Max remembered they had some sheets to cover the carpet to protect it from paint but was vague about where they might be now.

A search revealed them in the spare bedroom and gave the men two new problems. The sheets were under the stored furniture so they had to move that around to reach them, and then they realised they should've put the sheets down in the lounge prior to bringing their stuff in. So they improvised, trying to lay the sheets and moving their equipment as they went, not an easy task as it turned out and one that nearly cost Dickie his head.

Max held up one of the strong boards they had borrowed with the intention of placing it between two step-ladders so that whoever was painting the ceiling could stand upon it. He watched as Dickie spread the sheet where the board had lain, then turned his back on his partner when the operation was complete, an action that saw him swing the board around missing Dickie's head by millimetres as the man stood up.

Dickie decided he wanted a pee and in trying to negotiate his way around the dining room table wedged in the bathroom tumbled into the bath, thankfully empty of water. But the incident did produce the favoured Flemmdale expression 'O Buckett' or something similar.

Meanwhile Max had been busy setting up the step-ladders as they had now decided painting the ceiling was a job best completed first, and the accountant had reasoned that it might be to the good if they started at opposite ends and worked their way towards each other. They stirred their tins of emulsion and set off as agreed but climbing the steps Dickie misjudged his footing and fell to the floor, yet with great presence of mind concentrated his efforts on preventing the paint going everywhere. But success came at a cost.

He fell awkwardly and hurt his back.

There was nothing for it. The poor man's movements were restricted and he clearly could not go climbing again, so he started work painting one of the walls which was well within his revised compass. The point at which he started was perilously close to where Max was working overhead and he subsequently found himself with streaked hair which might have been more acceptable had it not been a mixed shade of topaz and mint green which did not complement his grey thatch at all.

During a mid-morning break taken on the now drying patio it became clear, especially to Max, that he would have to do the lion's share as Dickie could only cover the eye-level areas of the walls. Max suggested a massage might help and they went to the bedroom.

With great skill and deftness of touch, not to mention some soothing lotion, he eased Dickie's pain and raised his spirits to the point where the invalid became quite aroused, as did the nurse.

It was an hour before work resumed, but Dickie was now able-bodied again. Their enthusiasm was renewed and they tackled the decorating with vigour afresh.

"Why don't we have some music?" Max suggested.

"Know where the CD player is?" came the response.

"Not a clue."

"Well, that's that then."

"Yep, spose it is."

They continued without musical accompaniment.

Dickie dragged a pair of steps along the floor and dragged up the protective sheet at the same time. On the other end of the sheet was another pair of steps upon which Max stood. Foreseeing the inevitable accident Max called out:

"Dickie, me ol' sausage, watch what you're doing!" Dickie spun round just in time and prevented disaster much to Max's relief, but in spinning pulled the business end of his paintbrush across the wooden door frame.

"Oh dear," quoth he, "soon get that sorted. Never mind."

They'd decided they would have a fish and chip supper at a riverside restaurant they knew in Great Barsterd so there was the question of a lunchtime snack, and it was Max who headed for the kitchen to see what was available. In so doing he stepped unknowingly into a patch of paint on the sheet and then left footprints down the hall, while Dickie, having advised his partner of his transgression, followed with his cleaning materials.

Lunch, when the ingredients could be located, was comprised of salmon and cucumber sandwiches and a slice of lemon drizzle cake, all washed down with ice-cold San Miguel, and taken on the now dry patio where they placed a couple of chairs.

"Good morning's work that, Dickie," Max commented with a degree of assuredness and confidence that was horribly misplaced.

"Aye Maxie, and I reckon if push ever came to shove we could do this professionally. How does the name Thickwood and Forrest as a business sound to you?"

"Sounds more like we ought to be in timber or something," Max replied having pondered the possibilities.

"Shame about that window in the conservatory. Only just had it cleaned."

"Oh yeah, forgot that Dickie, Ernie being round first thing. Shame."

"Here Maxie, just looking into the lounge, have we made a mistake?"

"Whaddya mean me old fruit?"

"Weren't we going to have beige on the north and south walls?"

"Yep."

"Well, we've done 'em on the east and west."

The two peered into the room.

"O Buckett," Dickie exclaimed quietly and with resignation.

"O Buckett," Max echoed, with equal softness of voice.

At which precise moment Oliver Buckett drove past in his mini-bus en route for High Stayckes.

"O Buckett," chorused the pair as laughter overtook them.

"Right," said Dickie, "change of plan. We'll do north and south in Amber. Not got enough paint to re-start."

"No, and I don't know about you Max, but I ain't got any inclination to do so either."

"Agreed. Want another bottle Dickie?" Dickie studied his empty glass.

"Thanks but no. Let's leave it for afternoon tea."

And that is what they did.

The day passed without further incident and they cleared away much of their mess in plenty of time to get ready for their evening excursion. Tomorrow they could put everything back in the lounge and then tackle the bathroom. Sunday they had set aside for a grand clear out, not least of the garage which, like so many homes today, was a store of things needed and pointless clutter.

About the time they were settling down to their fish and chips (the restaurant also had San Miguel on tap) a neighbour was just starting her own evening pleasures.

Jade Mingo was dressing and dressing to kill. She might not have had youth on her side, being sixty-three, but she had a keen eye for a wardrobe that could show all that was still of value in a very good and appealing light. A redhead, her hair was always set in a provocative style, accentuating her facial features which in themselves were decorated to great advantage. Jade knew exactly how to apply her make-up.

Tonight she wore a loose-fitting yellow top, upper two buttons undone, that showed a tempting glimpse of her ample and well-rounded bosom. A tight, very tight, black leather skirt of very short proportions, with splits both sides, made up the next part of the picture, and standing where she could see her rear view in the mirror smiled with approval at the way the skirt clutched at her voluptuous bottom. The tops of her black fishnet stockings were just visible, as was a taste of flesh above, as were her red suspenders. She looked an absolute tart. Perfect! Ridiculously high heels finished the image. She admired her reflection, turning this way and that.

Man-killer, she gloated to herself. You still got it girl. Have any man you want!

Next she tidied the bedroom, skilfully adjusting the lighting and turning down a small corner of the duvet to reveal a hint of the black silk sheets within. Her pink baby-doll nightie was laid on the end of the bed.

How could it fail, she asked herself? The final touch was the bottle of champagne, well-chilled and set on a silver tray next to the two champagne flutes. She clapped her hands. Brilliant. A work of art perhaps?

And then there was the ring at the doorbell.

Jade hurried downstairs to meet and greet.

Within half an hour she was in the bedroom and lying seductively on her bed, lapping up the admiring glances, savouring every second of her success.

The cameras clicked away as members of the Flemmdale Amateur Photography Society took their pictures. Eva Longpoint was regarded as something of an expert by her fellow members and one or two sought her advice on angles and lighting. Ian Burge jumped about here and there with no fewer than three cameras around his neck while Society chairperson Dorothy Gimbald helped arrange and direct Jade's poses.

"Pity the bottle's empty," Barry Hindbush joked as he slanted his own camera up from the floor where he was lying in order to get a shot of Jade's face in the background with the champagne in the foreground.

Pictures taken the group descended the stairs with Dorothy in the lead ready to go to the kitchen to help with the refreshments that Jade's husband, Nick, had been preparing, leaving Jade to change into something more modest. She'd volunteered to take the modelling assignment for this shoot. On Sunday it would be Jason Tannick's turn taking the role of an angler down on the river, and they were all praying for good weather.

Jade would be there. She and Nick possessed an excellent piece of kit that was the envy of other members, a truly expensive camera that could do everything except make the tea so it seemed, and right now Jade was looking forward to seeing the photos her husband had taken of her. Later that night, when the visitors had departed, Nick praised his wife.

"You really looked the part darling. What are the chances of you dressing up like that again just for my benefit? Like right now?"

"Could you afford me pet?"

"How much do you charge?"

"Special price for you. A real bottle of champagne for a start."

"Funny you should say that. Just happen to have one chilling. A surprise for my own super-model."

"Well done Nick, and that's the right answer! I'll go and change. Did you really not mind me being such a model for the crew?"

"Not a bit of it. Proud to show you off. Might've made one or two jealous! How long have you had that costume now?"

"Oh donkey's years. You remember. Got it for that farce we were both in when we did amateur dramatics way back when." They both chuckled at the memory.

"Did you mind doing it Jade, I mean really, did you?"

"No because it's artistic, isn't it? Anyway that's my excuse and I'm sticking to it." More laughter.

"Besides, neither of us worried when Eva modelled that swimwear for all of us. We simply viewed her as artists view their models, didn't we? And, my cherub, my beloved, you were only being artistic getting behind her when she wore that bikini that was nearly cutting her bum in two."

"That's as cheeky as she was! Now I'd better get the champers before I get deeper into trouble!"

Laughter filled the room as she returned upstairs and Nick went to the kitchen. He glanced at some of his photos and said out aloud to himself:

"You looked lovely Jade. Now for the real thing….."

Chapter Fifteen

The moors and mountains of Countryshire stretch away to the north of Evelyn's Hole, rising steadily at first and then climbing sharply the further up the valley you look. At Evelyn's Hole the hillsides are gentle, the river itself, wide and more direct, flows through fertile plains, and the countryside, now less dramatic, is no less scenic.

Soon the Flemm will reach Great Barsterd. After skirting Evelyn's Hole it drifts past one last village, Gonn West, before arriving at the town. There is actually a Gonn East, located across the river, but it is barely a hamlet being comprised of four cottages well scattered. The word gonn is derived from a local dialect term for a bridge so presumably such a structure once existed here, although no record of it exists, but it might explain why there is a settlement both sides of the Flemm.

***

Gonn West

Gonn West has one claim to notoriety. It was host to the only murders committed in the valley in the last two centuries.

The heinous events took place in 1802. A villager named William Cunthrapp fell in love with a local lass called Harriet Heaver, but their union was not blessed, largely because William was married to somebody else and when Mrs Cunthrapp discovered the liaison she was less than pleased. Her husband overcame this small problem by drowning her.

There was too little evidence to prosecute William and a few months later he married Harriet. It was now that this farm worker diversified and started a new career development in forgery. When his employer, Farmer Balls, realised what he was up to William eradicated another difficulty in his life the same way he had dealt with the first. Balls was found floating face down in the Flemm.

100

Again, William Cunthrapp protested his innocence and again, there was little evidence to the contrary. However, Harriet was beginning to have doubts and was rightly concerned that she could be supplanted if her husband's attentions were diverted to a younger prospect. And she didn't fancy an enforced swim in the river by way of divorce.

William now worked for Balls's son who had taken over the farm. It so happened that Bowlock Balls had a handsome, comely wife Letitia whom William lusted after and so the route to disaster was set. Before Bowlock could drown, however, Harriet realised her peril and decided to take matters into her own hands, drowning Letitia in the customary manner.

Her husband was in the clear this time but evidence against Harriet was mounting. William could not let her take the blame and diverted attention by drowning Bowlock Balls anyway. That did the trick but he was now on the run. Nemesis arrived when he was arrested in Carlisle in connection with his efforts as a forger.

In due course he was hanged for defrauding the post office. History does not relate what happened to Harriet.

Gonn West is much safer these days. Property is quite dear given that it's a short way from town and that the road is straighter and wider than it has been coming south from High Stayckes, two aspects that make it attractive for those in Great Barsterd who seek the country life with easy access to their places of employment, education and entertainment. There are those who believe the lane should be taken at motorway speeds but there is a level of built-in traffic calming as there are often farm vehicles hogging the road, and occasionally herds of cows and flocks of sheep being moved about.

Add in the unpredictable movements of Oliver Buckett's bus, which never goes anywhere at speed, and car-racing has thus been effectively discouraged for the most part.

The Council approves a new-build from time-to-time, and there are a number of barn and dairy conversions in the area, so Gonn West is expanding and going some way to meeting housing demand.

The village is home to Flemmdale's oldest resident, Victoria Bunn, who was born in 1919 and who was the product of lust overcoming common decency when her father returned from the trenches and couldn't wait to get his hands, and other parts of his anatomy, on his lady friend.

A marriage was swiftly arranged as it had to be in those days.

Victoria's great-great-great grandchild Nola also lives in the village with her family and is sweet on a local boy, Peter. He writes her moving and beautifully illustrated love letters and she tells anyone who wishes to listen that Peter is the man she's going to marry.

As they are both nine years old it is likely to be a protracted courtship.

Love is at the root of a problem being experienced by another villager, Annie Handy. It is a long time since she was nine. She married childhood sweetheart cowherd Ethan Handy when she was nineteen but at the age of twenty-five has fallen for the charms of Julian Merry who has recently purchased a barn conversion just down the road. A large and attractive home indeed that set him back a pretty penny.

But then he has many pennies. A financial consultant based in Oddchester, where he lived prior to his move, he is able to work from home much of the time which has presented him with the opportunity to woo Annie. Her husband is very old-fashioned for a young man these days and he has no doubt been influenced by his upbringing in such a rural area. But he expected to provide for his new wife and did not anticipate her going to work, her role being to stay home and raise a family, of which there has been no sign, the pill proving successful.

Annie has deceived Ethan by pretending she is no longer taking the aforementioned tablets, but the time is coming when she really will have to give them up and get pregnant or her husband will insist on medical intervention and tests. Of course, the presence of Julian in her life is another reason for remaining on the pill for the time being.

Giving up her job in the petrol station shop, thus not having to travel to and from Great Barsterd, had substantial appeal to a fairly lazy nineteen year old, but over time boredom set in and she became ripe for plucking by a handsome, well-dressed, smooth-talking, smarmy, I-love-me-who-do-you-love, extremely wealthy city boy.

And as Ethan's working days were long the scope for misadventure was wide.

Looking after the farmer's cows was demanding employment. Up very early and not back home till late afternoon six days a week (although he came home for his lunch each day) meant that Annie saw precious little of him and when she did he was tired, so intimacy was infrequent and not very satisfying. After a couple of years as man and wife, and with no child on the way, he did relent and allow her to do a bit of domestic cleaning, and it was that medium that brought her to the attention of Mr Merry.

When he arrived he asked around for a house cleaner and was put in touch with Mrs Handy. And she lived up to her name in all respects.

Today being Saturday Julian was not at work but Ethan was. Annie was not due to be cleaning but was nonetheless at Julian's and since neither of them had any professional employment to pursue were lying in bed together.

"This is rather nice my little Annie," Julian simpered in his supercilious way, "as I expect Ethan's got his hands around some cow's tits and I've got mine round the best cow's tits in Gonn West." Annie giggled as she believed she was required to do although she neither appreciated his humour nor enjoyed being called a cow. He gently squeezed the object of his wit. She removed his hand.

"Don't call me a cow, Jules, it ain't nice, an' I don't like it."

"But you like me, my handy Annie, so you have to like the way I speak, and right now this bull wants to be taken to his cow," and he smothered her forthcoming objection with the most passionate kiss he could muster, a manoeuvre that won the day, Annie submitting to that which must be.

Afterwards, lying back on the pillow with a self-satisfied expression decorating his conceited face, he took Annie's displeasure to the next level by gloating about his conquest.

"How now Annie Cow? I think that's how the rhyme goes, doesn't it? And you're my handy cow, aren't you? How does it feel to be honoured being made love to by such robust stallion who can so easily satisfy your every desire?" She could scarcely believe her ears, and that was without analysing his curious mixture of bovine and equine creatures in his analogies.

"You wretched sod. Think you're doing me a favour do you….."

"Why of course I am," he interrupted, "and a favour much appreciated."

"You … you … you…"

"Yes? What? You're only the village cow and you can't do without me, so just be a good girl and do as you're told and take whatever I give you. And don't forget I've given you plenty of money which you've got stashed away somewhere. I don't suppose Ethan knows about that." He turned to face her. "Now handy Annie, my little cow, you don't want to lose that income and in truth you don't want to lose my body and the pleasure it brings you." He laid back on the pillow.

She was dumbstruck. Speechless. He'd never been like this before. He'd always been so charming and attentive, caring about her feelings, making her feel good about herself, and he'd given her spectacular sensations that were beyond her husband's abilities. Annie assumed she was something special to this man, that they met and loved on equal terms, but now she realised she was nothing more than a conquest, a convenient and fickle diversion, and had been used and abused.

The money had been accepted as a gift, but now she felt she'd been paid as a prostitute and she was filled with pain and revulsion.

"Well, that's it mate. I'm off, and I'll let you have every penny back, you bastard." She jumped from the bed and dressed hurriedly as he laughed at her and made moo-ing noises.

"Bye bye, little cow. Back to the arms of that dickhead. Let him please you if he can." Without another word she was gone but she was already plotting revenge as she threw the front door open and dashed along the road to her home.

In her own lounge she poured a can of Alfie into a glass, sunk the drink in one and poured another, still simmering with rage as she collapsed onto the settee, shaking with anger. The drink started to soothe the savage breast and she recalled an old saying 'revenge is a dish best tasted cold'. She was too worked up right now but she'd think of something.

First of all she went to her secret hiding place to gather up all the money she'd collected but saw to her absolute horror there was no money there. God, she thought as she clasped her hands to her face, has Ethan discovered it and taken it? And what might he have made of it? Oh God, she squealed out loud, it could only be Ethan. What the hell do I do now?

Her husband would be in for his lunch soon so she decided that for the moment preparing his meal was her priority, so she set to with vigour and presented Ethan with a dish fit to be placed before a king. Over their meal he made a sudden announcement.

"Haven't got to go back to work Annie, I'm done for the day. So I'm all yours." She made an immediate decision and waited until they were sitting in lounge with their cups of tea when the meal was finished.

"Ethan, I'm sorry, but I have something to say and I know I have to take the consequences whatever they may be." And she slowly told him the whole story and watched the sad little tears slip down his sorrowful face.

He stood up. She feared the worse. But he came and sat next to her and put his arm around her.

"Tis my fault. Don't pay you enough attention what with being at work and all. And yes I found the money but thought I'd wait until you missed it and told me about whatever it was. I'm sorry my darling. Will you give me another chance?"

Gawd, she thought, I'm the one who should be asking for a second chance. She told him so. They hugged and kissed and knew they would pull through okay.

Afterwards, tears dried and happiness restored, Ethan spoke.

"Now my darling, nobody calls my petal a cow and gets away with it."

"Oh Ethan, don't do anything silly please. Don't go and hit him."

"Not necessary. Got a much better idea. If you'll excuse me I think I'll go and see some real cows and, with farmer's agreement, borrow them for a while." She looked utterly baffled. "Don't worry precious. You an' me is forever. I'll not get into trouble, but I will deal with that buffoon, and we'll keep that money as a bonus!"

Annie had no idea what he had in mind but knew better than to either ask for an explanation or try to prevent him going out.

Half an hour later she heard a noise out the front and went to look through the window. She was astonished to see a herd of cows going by in the charge of Ethan and a mate and rushed to the front door to speak to her husband.

"Where y'going Ethan?" she called out.

"Just takin' this herd down to another field, that's all, won't be long." But something prompted her to keep watching, and sure enough when the cows reached Mr Merry's property Ethan accidentally on purpose ushered them up the driveway and into the garden where, being cows, they trampled over the lawns and plants eating whatever took their fancy on the way. Annie dashed down the lane to see what was happening and realised a small group of fellow villagers was assembling to observe the curious goings-on. She smiled. And then she smiled some more.

At which point Julian came hurtling out of his house.

"What the devil's going on here? Get them out. I'll sue you for everything," he bellowed.

"Can't 'elp it Mr Merry. You left yer gates open. You need to know more about country life. Not our fault me old son. And let's have none of this sue-age nonsense. Way of life up here, but you townies don't know that. Anyways, teach you to keep your gates shut, won't it?"

"I'll teach you a thing or two, you bloody yokel!" Julian roared at him as he struggled to get past the animals and reach his opponent.

The locals were cheering Ethan and the cows, and booing Julian.

Mr Merry reached Mr Handy and made a serious mistake. He landed the first blow, which everyone present bore witness to, and which gave Ethan the right of retaliation. Urged on by his wife and the small crowd, none of whom liked Julian or for that matter any of the haughty incomers, Ethan took his revenge, making a fearful mess of Mr Merry's face and leaving the consultant writhing in a freshly prepared steaming hot cow pat. Leaning towards the prostrate figure, now cowering lest further blows should fall, he spoke softly so nobody else might hear.

"That's what happens when you call my missus a cow. Don't you go suing anyone matey, or calling the police. Otherwise there might be worse in store for you." And with that the cows were rounded up and led back from whence they came while the onlookers laughed and cheered.

Another half hour passed before Mr Handy reached home where Mrs Handy greeted him with more hugs and kisses.

"You're my hero, Ethan. My hero. Stood up for my honour. Not that I deserved it....."

"Yes y'did my petal, and now I's going to make sure we have a happy life together. Come 'ere and let me kiss you again."

Julian Merry took care of his own wounds, swearing incredible oaths largely comprised of filthy language until he calmed down sufficiently to take stock of the situation. Yes, fair enough, he'd had his fun and he reckoned the villagers would make life hell for him if he pursued Ethan in any way, and he did quite like living where he was. Yes, best to leave well alone. He'd done all he wanted with that cow and enjoyed himself. Yes, leave it alone.

Nobody had any more trouble from him and a couple of villagers even came to help him put his garden to rights in the weeks ahead, so perhaps it was honours even.

And about fourteen months later Annie gave birth to twin girls which they named Natasha and Megan. Annie had abandoned the pill immediately after her reconciliation with Ethan and in due course nature did its bit. Hopefully it will be a case of 'and they all lived happily ever after'.

Chapter Sixteen

Our journey down the Flemm valley is nearly done.

Gonn West is the last village before Great Barsterd, although there are about ten miles of open countryside remaining with just an occasional building on the landscape.

We have travelled south from way up in the hills hearing many a tale as we have passed through the various settlements that make up this dalesland community, but now urban civilisation is upon us as this great river takes its rightful place as a prominent waterway heading for the sea via the city of Oddchester.

However, it may be fitting to end our story in Great Barsterd itself rather than on the open road in the middle of nowhere in some nameless place twixt the villages and the outer reaches of the built-up area. So we will make a final stop in the town that has featured in a few of the sagas, even though at a distance, and meet two of its entrepreneurs, Philip Everard and Vernon Cox.

***

Great Barsterd

From the sea the river Flemm was, for centuries, navigable as far as Great Barsterd, and certainly the wool merchants of the middle ages sent their materials onwards by ship from here. But many other items were imported and exported as trade thrived, the quaysides being eternally busy places, alive with the bustle of sailors, dock employees and trades people, and the constant coming and going of vessels.

Gradually, here as elsewhere, the river silted up and the railways arrived to take control of the movement of goods in bulk. The town suffered boom and bust, the wealthy wool merchants unable or unwilling to invest in the industrial revolution technology and consequently Great Barsterd went downhill fast.

Then German bombs took their toll during the second world war, but in the years that followed there was a slow upturn in the town's fortunes as new industries arrived and stayed and business flourished anew. More houses were built and mostly they were inexpensive for the era and that encouraged many folk to live in the area, even those that worked in Oddchester but could not afford property prices there. The motor car enabled people to travel more easily for employment reasons.

Now the town is up and running again, with much industry around and about, and a vibrant town centre with many shops. Most of the big supermarket chains have stores in the peripheral region, and suburbia extends in all directions, developers snapping up whatever land they can in order to make their financial killings. They'd build right the way up Flemmdale if they could but of that there is, thankfully, no hope, the valley being part of the Countryshire AONB.

Knowing the people of Flemmdale as well as he does it is no surprise that Oliver Buckett believes AONB stands for Area of Outstanding Natural Buggers.

Certainly there is an in-bred robust stubbornness about the country people, a blatant feeling of superiority over townsfolk, especially Barsterds (as residents of Great Barsterd are called), and a sense of pleasurable isolation from the worst effects of suburbanisation. Each village may seem ready to fight its neighbour if need be but nothing unites these scattered communities like a good fight with the town, or for that matter the rest of the country.

And the town looks up the valley and considers itself above the country bumpkins it assumes dwell there.

With all that in mind you might consider it curious that a son of the city should go into business with a son of the valley and that the enterprise be a success. But that is what happened.

Philip Everard was an Oddcestrian born and bred. His parents' sprawling house, with its two-acre garden and swimming pool in the outer suburb of Winkling, was where he enjoyed a head start in life. Father owned a large building company that had spread its tentacles across the region and beyond and he had amassed a fortune from it.

109

A private education followed, and thence university and a Masters in Social Statistics. The only problem was that Philip had no idea what he was going to do with his degree, or indeed what line of industry it might be useful in, and he didn't fancy local government or government at any level. By contrast Vernon Cox was born and bred in Sharpe Corner, the son of a farm-worker, educated at the Comprehensive which he left with precious few qualifications, but knowing exactly what he wanted to do. Not for him the outdoor life on a farm halfway up a valley whatever value the scenery might have.

No, Vernon Cox wanted to open a sex shop, but he had no idea how to go about it, and unsurprisingly no parental support. Quite the reverse in fact.

Then, by chance, he met Philip Everard. By now he'd all but given up his dream and was spending his days earning an honest bob or two with his father on the farm and hating every minute. He eschewed the concept of learning to drive and saving for a car. With what money he had he would occasionally take a taxi to town for an evening at a quiet pub in the company of an old school friend, Sandra Bunweed, who fancied him but was not to his taste.

He liked her company and witty conversation but that was all.

However, sometimes an opportunity comes about by the coincident timing of quite diverse activities, and on this evening three separate occurrences took place. First up Sandra took him to task once and for all.

"Look Ver, let's go back to my flat and do all kinds of adult things with each other. I don't arf fancy you, and you can do what you like, I'm dirty minded pet. And broad minded, if that's important. I'm wearing a thong that brings out the best in me bum."

"Sandy, you're a friend, a very good friend, it just doesn't feel right."

"Well, how about I tell you I've got a few sex toys, some battery powered. Would that excite you?"

"Sex toys? Where d'you get *them*?

"Oddchester. Not got anything like that in dreary old Barsterd. Give the oldies heart attacks round here, that would."

"Never told you this Sandy, but I've always wanted to open a sex shop ......"

"Hey, that's great Ver. Come back to my place and see some sample stock!"

"Yeah ..... yeah .... could do that I suppose." His reluctance was manifest in his speech.

"Make you a deal Ver. Come and have a look at my gear, I'll show you my gorgeous cheeks in this thong and we'll take it from there. If you don't want to stay and play, fine." She didn't mean the last bit but had great faith in her powers of temptation. She was confident she could get him to the starting gate with the chances of him escaping her reduced to nil.

"er .... mmm .... don't know ... oh well alright."

"Don't overdo the enthusiasm mate!"

At this juncture two men walked in. Philip Everard had forsaken the big city lights for dreary old Barsterd in order to visit a friend, banker Brandon Thetford, and the two had popped out for a convivial hour or so at Brandon's local.

By coincidence Brandon just happened to know Sandra who was presently at the bar getting the next round in.

"Sandra, you old devil, what brings y'here? Good to see you."

"Hi Bran, and not so much of the old. Good to see you and it's the promise of alcohol that brings me here. I'm with me mate Vernon over there." She could see the lecherous look in Brandon's eyes and sought to advise him she was fully booked for the evening. He looked disappointed.

"And Sandra, this is Philip. Told you about him. Got a Masters."

"Ooooo .... he can master me any time he likes!" she blustered hopefully in the other man's direction and was delighted to see from his face and body language that he'd accepted the signals and might be prepared to set his own at green.

"Good evening Sandra. Pleased to meet you," he simpered smoothly.

"What do you do Philip? Know old Brandon here's a merchant banker..."

"Not so much of that young lady," Brandon intervened, "I work for one of the high street banks as you know, or were you being rude? Anyway, Philip's looking for the ideal job right now. Managing Director, that sort of thing."

"Does he mean you're unemployed Philip?" All three laughed. "Well, yes, I am, but I can afford to look for the right opening. I want to get to the top so think I might as well start at the top!" More laughter, a little lighter this time. Brandon spoke.

"Philip says that, thanks to his degree, he could run any firm. He says you don't need to know anything about a particular business, just need to know how to run it, don't you Phil?"

"Ah Brandon, not quite as easy as that, but perhaps I shouldn't be that modest."

Sandra looked on in awe and admiration and asked the inevitable question.

"What's you Master in Philip?"

"Social Statistics actually." She decided against asking for an explanation believing it would all be beyond her anyway, and also concluded that asking how it would qualify him to run any firm would be pointless.

"That's interesting," she said instead. "My mate Vernon wants to open a sex shop. Could you run that Philip?" He sensed the sarcasm.

"Sounds boring to me Sandra......"

"Hang on Phil," Brandon interrupted, "how about it? Go into partnership with whatsisname and build it up into a major operation. Draw up a business plan and I'll get whatever finance you need."

Phil had endured his fill of sarcasm.

"Very funny....."

"No, no," cried Sandra who was almost jumping up and down, "I think it's a great idea. I've bought things at a sex shop (the mens' eyes were on stalks) and it's better than online, cos you can see all the things, get expert advice and all that. Loads of people use the shops, and lots more would if the idea was marketed right. There's a huge untapped audience out there. Money to be made." Brandon was laughing again, but he was alone. Philip was too busy thinking.

Growing impatient for his pint Vernon had wandered up to Sandra who now made the introductions and without drawing breath added:

"Brandon's trying to persuade Philip to go into business with you and open a sex shop. Start right here in Great Barsterd. You'd be the only shop of its kind. You'd make a mint, trust me, there's so many people out who'd love a sex shop on their doorstep." The three men looked sceptical. "If you're so good at everything, guys, like running a firm, you'll be good at marketing the project won't you? Start here in Barsterd and end up with a chain of shops everywhere."

The men were now looking everywhere except at Sandra and there was a pregnant pause. She spoke again.

"You're all bloody talk, aren't you? Big heroes. Listen, if you open a shop here I'll staff it for you, cos I obviously know a bit about it, what you need to stock, that sort of thing, and I'm not shy talking to people about sex."

The men could see that, no proof was necessary. Brandon sunk the rest of his pint and placed the glass on the counter.

"My round. Let's drink to this new project. How about it Phil? Don't tell me you wouldn't like the challenge? And you'd make a success of it, you know you would. Vernon's the man on the ground, Sandra can run the shop, and you can oversee the operation including development." Philip laughed but without humour and looked at farm-worker Vernon wondering just what he might bring to the table. Vernon realised Philip was seeing him as a dim yokel and decided attack was the best form of defence.

"Look Phil, I'm hard-working, work all hours, dedicated and thorough. You might say you got the brains and I got the brawn, but there's more than that. This is my dream and I know Sandy's right about the client-base. It's out there, boy, and we can grab a huge slice. All I ask is this: we're equal partners at all times and we have a proper legal agreement on that. And if we turns it into a company it'll be a private company with you and me as joint directors. I know you won't take me for a ride even though we've only just met. Gentleman you are. An' I'm a gentleman too even if it don't seem it, and I'm a mite cleverer than you could imagine." The look in his eyes made his position only too clear to Mr Everard.

113

"Right, we'll do it," Phil decided, "and there's no time like the present. Let's sit down and make some plans. Order some more drinks, my round, and we'll take them with us."

And from that small beginning, when the tiniest of acorns was sown, what was to become a mighty oak took shape as a frail infant that would require much nurturing in the months ahead before it could ever start to realise its lofty ambitions.

In due course the gang of four (Sandra was included at her insistence) made their plans and work started. Brandon ensured the business plan was approved by the bank and he also knew which palms to grease when it came to planning permission and licencing. Some Barsterds were horrified and objected but an astonishing number supported the scheme, Sandra and Brandon made sure of that. They featured in the local media to the shame of Vernon's mother who couldn't quite believe what was happening and that her son was involved.

The shock waves rocketed up Flemmdale where the news was greeted in a variety of ways, mainly public dismay, but privately it was treated in a salacious manner especially by the men, most of whom kept their approval quiet. One or two ladies were privately supportive but publicly condemned the outrage.

The partnership of Everard Cox came into being and in time officialdom nodded at the plans and a suitable property, near but not in the High Street, was acquired and converted once planning permission was granted.

Now it might be assumed that calling a sex shop 'Everard Cox' might actually be beneficial but Sandra objected at once.

"I want something softer myself."

"That must make you unique amongst women," Brandon scoffed but seeing the look on the woman's face added, "sorry Sandy, was only said tongue in cheek."

"Good. And if you ever want to get your tongue round my cheeks just ask." He didn't doubt she meant it.

Finally they settled for 'Sleepless Nights (adult fun centre)' and found a local minor celebrity to open it.

In the years that followed they opened more and more shops as the profits soared and Sandra was appointed an Area Manager. When the time was right they made it a private company with Phil as MD and Vernon as Chairman. Brandon could not be directly involved as a bank employee so he did the next best thing and married the effervescent Miss Bunweed in order to keep his hand in, and possibly other bits too.

The venture went from strength to strength and at long last Mrs Cox forgave her son his sins, welcoming him back in the family fold and even praising his success. Vernon's father had always been on his side but only on the quiet, for the mother had to be placated, soothed and brought round gradually.

Phil had no such parental difficulties, his father being fully supportive, his mother enthusiastic to the point where he thought she might even become a customer! He married a girl who might've earlier been beyond his reach and whose physical attributes far outweighed her mental ones, but who now saw serious money beckoning and made herself readily available. They moved into a palatial house on the outskirts of Great Barsterd where Chrissie gave birth to three children.

Vernon and Philip became millionaires but Vernon remained single acknowledging that he was free to play the field, and the field was full to brimming with eager maidens, and he had the money to do so. Why spoil it by falling in love with just one girl and, worse still, marrying her?

To date they have sixty-nine shops throughout the UK, sixty-nine being an apt number of course, and there are plans for more. Vernon still does the stock control and handles the day-to-day running of the affair, including hiring staff, while Philip manages the whole operation and is in charge of marketing.

All this came about by that set of curious circumstances: Vernon drinking with Sandra, Philip visiting Brandon and drinking in the same pub the same evening, Brandon knowing Sandra who just happened to mention Vernon's ambition.

And to this day nobody can understand how a degree in Social Statistics has helped Philip's achievements. Vernon's ceaseless endeavour has more than helped and the input from the switched-on Mrs Thetford has been a vital ingredient, such able assistance being occasionally overlooked by the MD of Sleepless Nights.

But he has had the last laugh, proving in his own eyes that he has made a fortune from successfully running a business he knows absolutely nothing about.

115

***

The Last Word

And so our journey ends.

Should you ever visit Countryshire do please explore the gorgeous Flemm valley and, who knows, you may even meet some of the characters you have read about, for many are still there.

There is a lovely constancy about the dale, personified by the old cottages in particular and the magnificent scenery abounding either side of the river (not to mention the area's history), yet it has embraced change as, it seems, everywhere must, but is doing so in a controlled manner in order not the spoil the overall appearance and atmosphere.

Do please support local trade – you'll have read about some of the businesses in the valley, the pub, butcher's, bed & breakfasts, cafe and so on, but a word of warning. Think twice about chancing your arm on the local bus service: Oliver Buckett's enterprise is still a mystery to locals and yet it survives.

Of course it is the appealing villages and the souls who dwell therein that make this area what it is. A rural community amidst some of the finest English countryside to be located anywhere.

Real people. Real souls.

Ah! …. Souls down the river indeed.

Author's afterthoughts

This story was instantaneously inspired by a TV episode of Paul Rose walking the Yorkshire Dales, in fact Swaledale. It was the inspiration but that is all; Yorkshire and the river Swale had no other part to play, for which they may be grateful!

Countryshire could be almost anywhere in England as long as there are hills and vales and rivers amidst some of the finest scenery to be enjoyed in the country. But it is a fictional county just as the plethora of settlements is obviously fictional.

The town and village names are imaginary but Britain is home to settlements whose real names are almost as seemingly ridiculous. For example: Pratts Bottom, Sewerby, Glenwhilly, Sinnington, Droop, Nether Wallop, Lickfold, Blubberhouses, Three Cocks, Over Peover, Crapstone, Bitchfield, etc., all really exist! As do dozens of other similar ones. A case of fact outdoing fiction.

None of the real ones would've been out of place in this book!

In chapter sixteen the banker is called Brandon Thetford; these are the names of neighbouring towns in East Anglia and their names just seemed to go together!

In chapter twelve there is a reference to asdic, an anti-submarine detection system widely used in WW2, and a form of sonar. If you're not familiar with it asdic (on a warship) pinged a signal into the water and received an echo if it hit anything solid. By this means it was possible to detect a sub, learn about its depth and course, and get into the best position to attack it with depth charges. An 'instantaneous echo' (the expression used in Chapter 12) showed the attacking vessel was right on top of its target.

Celine's views on slavery and racism (chapter 13) reflect the views of a dear friend, a Jamaican lady, with a similar background to the fictional Lady Faux-Parr and are therefore not my creation. The words are mine, but the views belong to another. I mention this simply as I would not wish readers to assume I was inappropriately expressing my own opinions on these subjects through another's lips.

Chapter 15 starts with the tale of murders committed at Gonn West in the early 19th century. William Cunthrapp's end on the gallows was inspired by the demise of the evil seducer in the saga of the *Maid of Buttermere*, a fact-based legend mentioned by Wordsworth and the subject of a book by Melvyn Bragg. It seemed to me that being hanged for defrauding the Post Office would be laughable today even if capital punishment still existed!

Finally, I must mention that I have been around many a long year, and it is always possible that some of my ideas have their roots in things I have heard or read in the distant past lying buried in the back of my mind. I would not knowingly stoop to plagiarism so apologise if any aspects of these stories may bear similarity to the work of others. It is not intentional and I hope that the entire book is totally original.

Other books by Peter Chegwidden

Peter writes across various genres so there's bound to be something for almost everyone. Many stories are based in Kent.

New work coming soon

THE MASTER OF DOWNSLAND

A drama set in north Kent during the 18th century

Disinherited for marrying the girl he loves David Grayan leaves family wealth and status behind. With what little money he has he embarks on various business ventures that eventually reap dividends and earn him his fortune.

He buys a handsome house in North Kent, and earns the respect of the country folk. But he is largely shunned by his own class particularly for his unconventional views and practices.

Then tragedy strikes.

His beloved wife, Marie, dies in childbirth. Unable to come to terms with his dreadful loss, he throws himself into his business affairs and retreats into a dark, solitary state where even his few close friends cannot help him, an emotionally broken man.

Then a new maid starts work at his Downsland Hall. But can a mere maid, a lowly servant, provide any medium by which he might emerge from his darkness into the light? And could he love again?

A dramatic tale of romance and love set against a backdrop of tragedy, family feuds, loyalty and betrayal, revenge, enduring and fickle friendships, bigotry and the constraints of society's conventions in the 18th century.

***

Books (e-books and paperbacks) available from Amazon now

The Chortleford Mystery

Murder comes to the Kent countryside and a quiet little unassuming village.

Everyone knew who the killer was, so why didn't the police *do* something?

A lovely old gentleman is slain in his back garden and everyone was sure his wicked stepson, Michael Martyn, carried out the dreadful deed. And Martyn has plenty of secrets he wants left hidden.

But it transpires there are other secrets in this rural settlement.

If you like your murder mysteries in a more genteel and cosy vein, tinged with humour, set in glorious bucolic surroundings, and with just enough sauce added to make it spicy, then this tale's for you.

No obscene language, no gory details.

Village gossip takes hold, the police seem baffled, a too-clever-by-half local reporter gets involved, and then, inevitably, another murder takes place. And secrets are uncovered.

One by one.

Death at the Oast

Another murder mystery set in rural Kent.

It being Sunday morning Audrey Modlum was playing golf and returned home to find her husband Gareth stabbed to death in the hall.

DCI Sheelagh Mehedren has little to go on. The last thing, the very *last* thing the DCI needs is an amateur sleuth sticking his nose in, but local octogenarian Ernest Pawden, a fan of TV crime drama, does just that. Animosity reigns, but gradually and begrudgingly her attitude towards him softens.

Could a truce be in the offing? And could it lead to the killer?

Unbeknown to all of them this is vital as an innocent lady is in the killer's sights and time is of the essence.

Like the popular *"Chortleford Mystery"* by Peter Chegwidden this story is written in a similar cosy vein, with humour and a degree of gentleness, with the added ingredients of satire, pathos, poignancy and just a little sauce.

The tale is as much about the diverse characters and developing events as the murder!

No Shelter for the Wicked

Three unexplained, seemingly motiveless murders in different parts of the country. No clues, no murder weapons, no meaningful DNA, no useful forensic evidence. Nothing to connect them.

Then the police discover a bizarre and tenuous, wafer-thin link. But how to progress it with nothing to go on? Or is it all coincidence? The police don't think so.

A private eye, an ex-cop, doesn't believe in such coincidences either. He's a suspect in one of the murders, and by chance he becomes more deeply involved in the investigations. In a remarkable set of circumstances he forms an unlikely alliance with a supposedly disreputable woman, an ex-con, who is desperately seeking her sister, and they set out on a quest that eventually leads to peril. And a terrible shock for this woman he has befriended.

The trail heads from Kent to Hertfordshire, Suffolk, the Derbyshire Dales, north Devon and the Lake District, and eventually to a life or death situation and heartbreak.

A tale of murder, mystery, of love and passion in many guises, of deceit, betrayal and vengeance, played out across the country as the tension mounts inexorably towards its horrifying climax.

Peter Chegwidden has written a crime novel of many separate threads entwining as the thrilling denouement approaches, and has done so with his own style of humour and pathos, satire and poignancy.

Kindale

It is the late 18th century, in the reign of George III. Major events such as the American War of Independence, the French Revolution and the Napoleonic Wars belong to this era. Indeed even now Napoleon is rising to power.

The fear of war is bringing uneasiness to Kent as it is elsewhere.

Now the mysterious Oliver Kindale is on his way to Dover.

His destiny is aligned to the activities of a Frenchman and an English outlaw. Threatening developments in France seem to be at the centre of his critical mission. But Kindale is not an officer of the law, nor is he a military man. Indeed, little is known about him.

The east Kent coast has been a hotbed for smuggling but Kindale is not pursuing the free-traders, although their paths will inevitably cross. Which side of the law does Kindale operate on? What are his motives? Why is he in Kent at all?

And what of the man himself?

Death hangs in the air. These are dangerous times and Kindale will face danger and other challenges, some that will test him heart and mind, body and soul.

Could the very fate of England be in his hands?

Tom Investigates

This is intended to be a simple, charming little fun story about cats.

These cats are not cartoon cats, or any sort of animated cats, they are just the neighbourhood cats we come across every day. Perhaps even your very own cat! They are cats behaving like cats just as we see them behaving every day. But in this tale we allowed into their world. We hear them speak and learn what they are thinking.

It is a kiddies tale for adults. Just sit back, relax and enjoy!

Admittedly the adventures are very far-fetched but otherwise there would be no story. There are several interwoven threads and several very happy endings.

There is no bad language or anything to offend.

So come with us and get in touch with your feline side.

Tom Vanishes

The sequel to Tom Investigates sees the tabby accidently kidnapped and taken from the Isle of Sheppey to a mainland supermarket.

The story follows Tom and his efforts to get back home. His feline discover by chance what has happened and devise plans for his rescue with chaos ensuing.

Along the way Tom strikes up an alliance with a stray cat that will lead him into unforeseen difficulties. Meanwhile the Minster Moggies get themselves into all kinds of tangles as their rescue operations founder.

So is there a happy ending? Of course there is, well, several in fact.

Tom Vanishes is available as an e-book only.

Sheppey Short Stories

Eighteen short stories all based on Kent's Isle of Sheppey about the year 2014.

All kinds of tales from the humorous to the sad, the satirical and the ghostly, the romantic and the saucy, tales of heroism and tales of despair, but mostly stories to warm you. Great fun!

Here's one of them, entitled: **Gerald and Sylvia** – *a tale of a turning worm*

Meticulous planning.

Gerald's whole life had involved meticulous planning. He relied on it. It had brought him success at work, success in almost all his leisure activities, and it had brought him success in wooing Sylvia.

In fact, courting Sylvia had been like the execution of a military operation. Target: marriage. Go, go, go.

The strategy had worked a treat. And like the implementation of all great military manoeuvres he had had every avenue accounted for, ready to cope with setbacks (of which there were very few), and retained a plan B just in case.

Plan B was Barbara, but Barbara wasn't needed. Plan A came up trumps.

So it was essential that when arranging and participating in a holiday Gerald had everything mapped out, every eventuality covered, and a back-up plan at every stage along the way.

Sylvia tolerated what she termed his eccentricities although she had never voiced such terms, nor ever hinted that he might possess such idiosyncrasies.

She was altogether a tolerant woman.

They suited each other. Up to a point.

Sylvia was born in Maidstone and grew up there but had moved with her parents to Borden, just outside Sittingbourne, by the time she met Gerald. He came from Doddington although he was little more than an infant when his own folks moved up the road to Faversham.

Their path to Clovelly Drive in Minster had been winding and twisting but both felt they had 'come home' at last. They had previously dwelled in Rainham, Hollingbourne, Bapchild, Lynsted and Iwade but not necessarily in that order, although they moved to Sheppey from Iwade as that village grew and grew and grew. Grew, but not nicely, in Gerald's opinion.

Since Gerald's opinion was the only one that counted in their marriage it was only a question of time before such nomadic people would choose to up sticks and set sail yet again.

At long last they had found their true home up a crumbly unmade road. Presumably the way Minster had grown, *was* growing, was entirely to Gerald's satisfaction. Sylvia said not a word, so nobody, least of all her husband, knew what she really felt about it all.

His employment was currently in Canterbury and his daily commute usually brought no comment whatsoever, save when there was a delay at the bridge either way, in which case there would be vociferous and hearty condemnation of people in authority, especially the police and the council, over dinner in the evening.

His wife tolerated his outpourings, grateful that no unpleasant language infiltrated his discourses. Her role was to say yes and no in the right places, offer sympathy where it was clear it would be welcome, indeed vital, and to try and avoid making any adverse observations, least of all in defence of the police and the council.

Happily there were more days when Gerald could work from home. Ah, technology! His 'office' was one of the bedrooms and Sylvia had privately named it the Enterprise after the Star Trek starship. She thought his office looked like a flight deck, so much technology. He could even do what he told her was video conferencing, but she believed it had another name now, one she had not been informed about.

No matter. None of her business anyway.

Right now there was the holiday to look forward to.

The Lake District. Gerald had chosen the destination. He always did. He had selected the hotel. He always did. And he would be doing the driving.

He always did.

That meant he chose the route and the stops. But none of this organisation would've been worth a light had Sylvia been excluded. His wife was expected to pack and ensure that everything they could possibly need was packed, not forgetting the first aid kit or the walking sticks, and that there was plenty of clean clothing. Better to bring clothes back unworn than not have them when required while away.

So Sylvia toiled away, checking the 'kit' as she called it, counting underpants and knickers, making sure socks a-plenty were in matching pairs, and convincing herself they would have clothes for all weathers and all occasions. Washing, washing, ironing, ironing. Then there were the shoes, boots and slippers. Clothes to be folded and neatly placed in suitcases so that all available space could be maximised.

She sang, hummed, from time to time whistled, and just carried on uncomplainingly with her chores, for that was her lot, and she could leave all else to Gerald.

She had never been organised person. Neat and tidy, yes, disorganised definitely. Clean and tidy, most certainly. Meeting her future husband had been such a boon. He'd taken so much weight of responsibility off her shoulders and given her so much freedom from worry. So kind, so understanding, he'd been magnificently supportive and always so sweet and attentive.

From the earliest days of their marriage he had helped her no end by gradually removing all the things that seemed to concern her, and laying them upon his own burden so she should not be troubled and was free to enjoy life. Why, he had patiently explained that she didn't need the worry of her own bank account, let alone having to sort out the bills, so all their income went into his account and he attended to all household finance.

Yes, Sylvia was relieved about that. And he was always so very generous with her housekeeping money. No worries there! She had often wondered if she should ask if he was coping with everything but knew he wouldn't appreciate it. He was the man of the house and on him was sat the yoke of domestic responsibility in all matters. It suited her, she had all she wanted, and was content.

It was so useful to have such a well-organised, meticulous and fiscally sound man about when she was pregnant and bringing up their two children. There was never any question of her returning to work and none now long after the chicks had flown the nest.

So Gerald worked hard and now occupied an executive post. Sylvia, housewife and mother, had raised their brood and kept the marital home and did all things required of an obedient and subservient wife. Her acceptance of her role seemed to please her husband.

She never asked about the finances, never knew what he earned, had no idea how much mortgage was involved buying their dream home in Clovelly Drive, knew nothing of the household bills, and quite naturally assumed he was entitled to enjoy the big, black Mercedes he drove. It was his dream car, he'd explained, but Sylvia couldn't help thinking it was a case of boys with toys. Anyway, she was happy pottering around in the little Nissan he'd bought her.

A car's a car, she'd reasoned, something for getting around in, from the proverbial A to B, something that need not be expensive to run. He'd informed her the Nissan wasn't, and she'd always found it very economical. She bought petrol from her generous housekeeping. In fact she paid cash for everything as she didn't have the inconvenience of a credit or debit cards.

Evil things, Gerald had explained, although, she knew, he possessed several himself. Essential for a businessman she was told. Essential for today's confident and self-assured executive. Gerald seemed to have everything that such a person should possess, not least golf club membership and friends in high station.

Presumably a mistress was part of the complete package.

Sylvia had found out about Evelyn quite by chance. A fellow golfer. One summer's day, the weather being delightfully warm, Sylvia had walked into Sheerness. Gerald was at his office in Canterbury or so his wife thought. Except that he wasn't.

Taking the footpath from Scrapsgate to Halfway she was astonished to see his Mercedes in the golf club car park. But not half as astonished as she was to be moments later. Looking back she happened to see Gerald and a woman wheeling their golf bags towards his car. They were laughing together and when Gerald suddenly stopped and put his arms around her and kissed her lips Sylvia ducked behind a bush to watch rather more covertly.

Both golf bags went into his boot and the woman climbed into the passenger seat. They exchanged what looked to Sylvia like a lingering kiss. Then they moved closer and appeared to be making a much better and prolonged fist of sharing a more meaningful kiss.

Sylvia's legs turned to jelly. Shortly her husband and his lady friend drove right past where Sylvia was concealed and Sylvia was physically sick. Somehow she found her way home, laid on the bed and sobbed. Then something curious happened. She found herself asking why she was crying, and began to realise she was doing what convention demanded rather than acting fully out of emotional distress, despite the shock.

Pulling herself together she decided to look around. Gerald's office, the small bedroom, was the obvious place to start. Drawers were locked. That was another nasty little shock, a husband locking things away. But perhaps they were private business matters that were truly none of her business? She was confused and discovered she was inventing all kinds of excuses when perhaps none were needed, for surely he would leave no evidence at home?

She took a folder from a shelf and sat down at his desk. Inside were current account bank statements, the latest right on top, and Sylvia's eyes bulged. What she quickly realised were his salary payments seemed to her to be mammoth, extraordinary sums of money. But she couldn't understand all the regular payments, and had no idea what some of the cheques were for as they were quoted as numbers only, no recipients names.

There was, however, one quite large monthly payment to an Evelyn Pannell arranged by direct debit, same amount every month. Big money, even by Sylvia's standards, but not a big chunk out of that salary by any means.

Further investigation proving fruitless she returned to the lounge and did something very unusual indeed. She poured herself a drink. Even more unusual it was a very large scotch, for Sylvia rarely touched spirits. But it was from his treasured bottle of Islay single malt and she had no compunction now in depriving him of a good few mouthfuls.

She decided to say nothing when he returned home. Why rock a smooth sailing ship? So she bided her time and continued playing the dutiful wife and took advantage of every opportunity as it presented itself to discretely check up on her husband. In fact it was a couple of months later that the gods smiled upon her and she had the chance to go through his mobile's contact list and there, sure enough was E's mobile number and her work number.

Thus it was that Sylvia discovered that Evelyn Pannell worked for another Canterbury based company.

The pieces of the jigsaw started to slot together and over a period of time Sylvia was able to deduce that Evelyn lived on Sheppey, probably also in Minster, and arrive at some other facts her husband and his mistress would probably have preferred to keep secret.

And still she said nothing. She had learned an important lesson, namely that she had great affection for her other half but didn't feel anything approaching love in any sense of the word. If truth be told they were little more than companions and the situation did at least explain why the physical side of their relationship had dried up. She was far from heartbroken. Far from.

So life continued as before as if nothing had happened.

Of course, she concluded, that is why they had to move to Minster! And by now Sylvia had Evelyn's home address, not that she intended to visit or anything like that. Confrontation with Gerald or Gerald's mistress was out of the question. Not her style. Let him play his games, for one day even a worm will turn.

Now she was packing for their holiday. Ullswater and Glenridding. What a lovely lakeside setting. Delightful walks. She remembered from way back when that you could take the steamer across the lake and walk back along the banks. Delightful. And she allowed some delightful fantasies to make merry in her imagination. Gerald falling overboard, his body never found. Gerald falling down a mountain. They had, in their youth, walked right up to the peak of Helvellyn from Glenridding, following in the footsteps of so many keen walkers. Could she persuade him to go again? And not come home alive?

No, that was just nasty, and, after all, she would rather he and Evelyn perished in each others arms! Or, more lovely still, that Evelyn should strike a golf ball with such velocity that, as it hit an unsuspecting Gerald in the head, it killed him outright. Then, overcome with grief, Ms Pannell would take an overdose.

And with those charming thoughts to warm her Sylvia settled down to a tot of Laphroaig. Her husband never noticed his favourite single malts were being thus attacked. She had already assisted him in devouring a Lagavulin and an Ardbeg and had developed quite a taste for the peaty whisky, going so far as to suggest they revisit Islay in the not too distant future.

An inebriated Gerald drowning in a vat of whisky had at one time been her principal dream.

She enjoyed watching old episodes of the tv detective *Colombo* as many of his criminal adversaries felt they had concocted the perfect crime, normally murder. And she dreamed freely of how she might bring about the demise of Gerald and Evelyn in one fell swoop.

Sylvia discovered there was a Mr Pannell, but it was extremely unlikely he was benefiting from the monthly income being provided by Mr Meticulous Planner. Where was the money going? Were they building up a nice little nest egg to give them a start in life? In the Pannell household, so she learned, it was Mr Pannell who was the breadwinner, or rather the goose that laid the golden eggs for Mrs Pannell, who, let it be said, had a very menial and lesser paid position.

Mr P was a property developer, Mrs P was an admin assistant.

Sylvia had consulted a solicitor who reckoned that, in the event of divorce, she might end up with the lions share as she had no money of her own. Yes, she was technically co-owner of their Clovelly Drive home, and she should surely be able to afford a decent homestead should it come to divorce. But what of Mrs Pannell? Did she have most to lose? Was Gerald providing her with the means to walk out on Howard Pannell? Puzzles, puzzles.

All purely academic, she mused, if both met with a fatal accident.

There was another reason why Sylvia had adopted a rather carefree attitude to her husband's infidelity, notwithstanding the financial aspect or the fact there was so little love. What was good for the gander being good for the goose Sylvia had taken a lover.

Nigel was quite a bit younger and he was fit in every sense, and free from any current attachments. Handsome, charming, courteous, generous, kind and caring, he himself had been smitten and flattered by the elegant Sylvia. Attractive woman, home in Clovelly Drive, great clothes, great dress sense, class, breeding, quality, good fun to be with, whisky drinker!

He was beside himself when Sylvia took an interest in him. For her part he was going to be her *Lady Chatterley's Lover*, a 'bit of rough' as she believed the terminology was. He wasn't one of life's great workers but found some employment here and there mainly as a barman, and it was in one such spell of work that he met his 'lady of the manor' and charmed his way ultimately into her bed.

He thought he had done well, but Sylvia let him think that. She got what she wanted.

She would miss him while she was away in the Lake District.

However, events were about to overtake the holiday preparations.

Sylvia had grown accustomed to spying and covert operations where her errant husband was concerned and over the months never lost an opportunity to explore his supposedly secret world. And so it was that she chanced upon a couple of documents that led her to believe Gerald and his beloved Evelyn were up to mischief in a criminal sense and were not merely content with extra-marital activities. A broad grin fell across her face. Mischief could be a game for any number of players! Being a law abiding citizen herself she put her marital obligations to one side and did her duty (as she saw it) by taking the documents to the police who were most interested.

Of necessity her home had to be thoroughly searched, and around about the time Gerald and Evelyn were arrested, but Sylvia was still grinning, admittedly to herself. Her husband was seething with rage when they finally met and that only made her grin wider and more public.

Divorce! Divorce! He had yelled the words at her and she had smiled all the more and taken his temper to the next level by asking meekly if the holiday was off.

She wasn't in court when he and Evelyn were committed for trial on charges of money laundering and fraud.

Granted bail he returned home and found it deserted. No meal ready. None of his washing done. Dust on the dining table. He also found Sylvia's handwritten note.

"I know you want a divorce. My solicitor tells me that, given our relative positions, and the evidence I have given him, we should be able to take you to the cleaners. In fact, I think you'll glow in the dark. I have gone on holiday with my friend to break one of the Ten Commandments and many times over. Isn't adultery exciting? Of course you know that, but difficult to commit in prison I dare say. It'll be much easier for me on the isle of Islay with my friend. Thanks for sharing your scotch with me. I'll raise a glass to your memory, a glass of one of your favourite tipples.

"This worm has turned."

Sheppey Short Stories is available as a e-book only.

Deadened Pain

A parody of the crime novel genre

The story starts with the investigation into a robbery at a local garage, in which very little was taken, and gradually gathers momentum as the crimes become more serious and involve kidnap and murder. It is only as the tale unfolds that the very serious nature of some of these crimes and their terrible connections and consequences become apparent.

Detective Chief Superintendent Luke Fuselage works for Birkchester CID and it is probably as well for the good citizens of the area that serious crime is rare if this particular DCS is the best they have. However, things are about to change and more dramatically than anyone could've imagined. In a quiet village a long way from town a body is discovered, a body that is horribly mutilated. Thus starts to unravel an extraordinary chain of events that will test the local police force to the limits as the body count increases, and result in a race to find a killer or killers before he, she or they strike yet again.

Sound familiar? Yes, it's the stuff of all good crime fiction, naturally. But most crime fiction doesn't feature someone of DCS Fuselage's ability at the helm. There are red herrings, and probably some of different hues, and there are twists and turns. All sorts of characters wander in and out of the story. Unsurprisingly.

Join Fuselage on this voyage into the dark unknown as he pieces together the clues that will lead him to the perpetrator. But first he must find and identify those clues. It's a case that will require all his ingenuity, experience and expertise. And somebody is keeping one step ahead of him and seemingly outwitting his team at every opportunity.

And his squad has all the elements that are needed in any successful team: togetherness, love, loathing, jealousy, incompetence, admiration, stupidity, efficiency, cliques, aggression, shyness, lust, sensitivity, contempt, cleverness, nastiness, cunning.

The private lives of some of the police officers become caught up in the story as each person is swept along by their own emotions and events at work. Fuselage's team is comprised of a curious mixture of personalities all bubbling along in their own ways trying to achieve an ultimate goal. As matters get worse additional members are drawn into this team and it seems that there could be an internal issue none has bargained for.

Expect the unexpected. The unimaginable can be the reality. The truth may be startling.

Deadened Pain is available as an e-book only.

Printed in Great Britain
by Amazon

80842827R00078